· BOOK I ·

Bayshore Medical Center Series

Andrea Whitman: Pediatrics

Stephanie Gordon Tessler and Judith Enderle

WALKER AND COMPANY, NEW YORK

To Andrea Brown with love and thanks

Special thanks to Carol Drago, R.N., Pat Haynes, R.N., and Marti Roth, R.N., John Zmiejko, M.D., Mariann Zmiejko, and other medical professionals who took time to answer questions.

First published in the United States of America in 1983 by the Walker Publishing Company, Inc.

Published simultaneously in Canada by John Wiley & Sons Canada, Limited, Rexdale, Ontario.

ISBN: 0-8027-6507-6

Library of Congress Catalog Card Number: 83-6949

Printed in the United States of America

10 9 8 7 6 5 4 3 2 1

Library of Congress Cataloging in Publication Data

Tessler, Stephanie Gordon.
    Andrea Whitman, pediatrics.

    (Bayshore Medical Center series; bk. 1)
    Summary: Andrea, a Nurse-in-Training in the Pediatrics ward of Bayshore Medical Center, finds life in the ward hard enough without the teasing of technician, Joe Duffy, especially as he can't compare with the impressive head of Pediatrics, Dr. Stewart.
    [1. Nurses—Fiction. 2. Hospitals—Fiction]
I. Enderle, Judith A. II. Title. III. Series.
PZ7.T286An 1983   [Fic]   83-6949

1

Handy Andy,
the Cowboy, and
Dracula Joe

HE COULDN'T HAVE gone far, could he? Andy wasn't so certain as she rushed from room four, leaving Heather and the rat-a-tat laugh of television's Woody Woodpecker behind. She looked up and down the long hospital corridors. At first she saw nothing, then a quick glimpse of disappearing black curls and a pair of red fringed pajamas caught her eye. There he was. She ran, waving as she passed the pediatric nurses' station. There was no time to stop and ask for help. The open-mouthed, surprised look of Mrs. Wernick, the head nurse on duty, barely registered as she sped by.

She skidded to an abrupt halt a few feet beyond Mrs. Wernick's desk. Her white nurses' shoes left a colorless mark on the highly polished vinyl floor.

Robbie Washington, who along with his roommate, Heather Berk, was supposed to be engrossed in cartoons, was standing in front of the third-floor elevator doors, patiently waiting for them to open.

A smile slowly spread over Andy's face as she looked at the pint-sized, runaway cowpoke. How could anyone get mad at such an adorable child? Even if he was more of a handful than any other three kids his size? Caring for Robbie was a big job. The doctors were trying as diligently as was humanly possible to regulate his medication, but Robbie's epileptic seizures continued. They were becoming fewer and less severe, but they were a fact of his young life. He shouldn't be out of his bed alone, without a doctor's permission and without supervision, but he was—constantly.

"Okay, partner," Andy said softly to the PJ-clad cowboy in the boots, one-gallon hat, and holstered six-shooter. "Time to mosey on back to the old homestead." She knew from experience that rounding up Robbie was a skittish job. So she played his game, trying not to alarm him and cause him to run again.

"I don't wanna," shouted Robbie; his large, dark eyes flashed Andy their challenge. He was like an unbroken pony, who, smelling freedom just over the next hilltop, bolts away, hooves flying. He was off again. For a small boy of six, he could run like a streak of lightning.

"Robbie Washington, you come back here," Andy shouted. "I'm getting awfully tired of chasing you. Robbie!"

Without slowing his gallop at all, Robbie pulled out his toy gun and began shooting at Andy over his shoulder. "Gotcha. You can't catch me," he called. Then, as abruptly as his stampede had begun, Robbie pulled in the reins and stopped.

It took a long moment before Andy realized why Robbie had stopped running. Coming slowly up the corridor, pushing his lab cart, was pesty Joe Duffy, one of the part-time phlebotomists on the pediatric floor. Robbie was trapped between them. "Howdy, Rob. What's the big hurry?" Joe asked him.

"I'm leaving," answered Robbie, defiantly placing his hands on his hips and staring up at Joe and then back at Andy, who gasped for breath behind him. He seemed undecided about which direction he should run.

"Are you now? And is Sheriff Whitman escorting you out of town?" Joe asked him. Like everyone else who worked on the pediatric floor, Joe was aware of Robbie's condition and the unpre-

2

dictability of his seizures. Joe seemed to have tuned in to the situation immediately.

Taking advantage of Joe's having Robbie's undivided attention, Andy began to move in. Slowly she inched her way toward her runaway charge. But her sudden lunge for Robbie made him spring in the opposite direction to avoid her grasp. Now Robbie found himself tucked tightly into Joe's arms, where his leap had unexpectedly put him. And Andy's effort to sneak up on the escaped cowboy ended with her sprawled across the tile floor at Joe's feet. Her starched white cap was lopsided, her brown curls disheveled, and she felt a sharp, stinging sensation in the seat of her pride.

"Hey. Put me down," demanded an indignant Robbie.

"Nope. I don't think so. It's my duty as a law-abiding citizen to see that you're turned over to the proper legal authorities."

"Would you mind . . . ?" Blushing and embarrassed by her less than graceful landing, Andy reached up for Joe's assistance.

"Let me go! Let me go!" insisted Robbie, struggling to get loose.

"Hold on, partner. First I gotta pull this prickly ol' sheriff out of her cactus patch," teased Joe, a delighted twinkle lighting up his sky blue eyes.

Prickly! Me? Prickly? His unsuppressed grin made her pull back her hand. She saw nothing humorous about having fallen at Joe Duffy's feet. He was always teasing and joking, the Funny Phlebotomist. She didn't find him amusing, and she wasn't the least bit impressed. Medicine was serious business, and Mr. Duffy didn't know the meaning of the word "serious." She certainly didn't want or need his help—or his sense of humor. As she yanked her outstretched hand away, she slipped back to the floor with a thud.

"Very prickly," Joe repeated, shaking his head.

"Oh, you . . . Joe Duffy . . . you!" Andy muttered, feeling the heat of her renewed embarrassment creep over her cheeks.

"Let me, Andréa," said a resonant voice, pronouncing her name as if it belonged to a Greek goddess—An-*dray*-a. That exciting voice could belong to only one person: Daniel Stewart, M.D., head of pediatrics—mature, kind, wise, all the best qualities a really fine doctor should possess. And Dr. Dan was handsome, too.

3

"Thank you, Doctor," she mumbled, taking his offered hand. Andy wished she could suddenly become invisible. She worried about what he saw as he stared down into her flushed face, and she prayed that he hadn't felt the shiver than ran up her arm when his warm fingers closed around hers. "I—I know this must look terrible . . . me on the floor. . . . But, I can explain. I. . . ." On her feet at last, she smoothed her fitted top and brushed off the pants of her uniform. Pretending a casualness she didn't feel, she reached up and straightened her cap. She didn't need to be told that her usually rosy pink cheeks were closer to American Beauty red.

"No, no, Andréa. There's no need. I'm sure I can guess how all this happened. Can't I, Robbie?" The doctor's question made Robbie duck his head against Joe's shoulder and smile sheepishly. "I'll bet you were headed for the pony rides again, right?"

"Uh-huh," Robbie whispered and nodded.

"Well, how about Ol' Doc Dan giving you a big pony ride all the way back to your room? Sound good?"

Robbie held out his arms eagerly. A bright smile lit up his face.

Andy admired the way the head of pediatrics charmed the small boy into his arms and gained his confidence. She and Joe walked together behind Dr. Dan as he carried the thrilled Robbie back to his room in a bouncing horseback ride. The happy ripple of the child's laughter filled the corridor and Andy's heart.

"What that kid really needs is a good talking to—on his bottom," whispered Joe, pushing his cart beside Andy. "Playing pony rides will only encourage him to take off again when the mood strikes him."

Andy stared at Joe unbelievingly. How could anyone that unfeeling work on the pediatric floor? And how dare a mere phlebotomist like Joe Duffy question the actions of a doctor as talented as Daniel Stewart? "Then it's a good thing that Dr. Dan is in charge, and not you, isn't it?" She began walking faster, forcing her gaze to return again to the horse and rider in front of her.

She lengthened her step, and her increased speed brought her to the doctor's side. She felt the familiar flutter that standing close to Daniel Stewart always gave her. Even though Andy was nearly five

4

feet six, standing next to the doctor, who was six feet two, hair slightly silvered at the temples, so mature, so attractive, made her feel petite, almost delicate. Next to a man like that, Joe Duffy was a nerdy child. If anyone needed a good talking to, he did!

"Wait out here a minute, will you, Joe?" asked the doctor, when they reached room four.

Andy pushed past Joe's cart and followed Dr. Dan to the empty bed in the room Robbie shared with five-year-old Heather.

Heather peeked out between the side bars of her bed and looked at Robbie with a worried expression.

"Here he is, Heather," announced Andy. "Safe and sound."

"Is Robbie bad? Are you going to hit him?" Heather's voice had a terrified edge to it. She seemed very close to tears.

Andy was startled by the question, and by the little girl's look. She couldn't help noticing the frown that creased the doctor's forehead.

"Robbie isn't bad, Heather," he said. "Maybe a bit too mischievous."

"Robbie's just like Curious George, the monkey. Isn't he? From now on, Heather, shall we call him Curious Robbie?" Andy began removing Robbie's cowboy gear while he sabotaged her efforts by giggling and wiggling about.

"Robbie's Curious George," said Heather, smiling again.

"You tickle, Andy. Can I keep my gun in bed?" Robbie's big round eyes were all the coaxing she needed. "I need it to shoot all the bad guys," he told Andy, eyeing her, Dr. Dan, and Heather suspiciously.

"If you don't go away again without me, Robbie, I'll let you shoot me—all you want," Heather offered magnanimously.

"Okay. Sure," replied Robbie nonchalantly.

Andy handed over Robbie's shootin' iron, and he took aim at her.

"Don't shoot, Quick Draw," she joked, putting up her hands in mock surrender.

"I wouldn't really shoot you, Andy."

"Just me . . . and the bad guys. Huh, Robbie?" Heather said proudly.

5

"Yeah. Just her," he confirmed. A real bond of friendship seemed to have formed between him and the adoring little girl who had checked in that morning, in preparation for her tonsillectomy. "And, Mrs. Grymes," he added with a grimace. It was obvious that Robbie was not as favorably impressed with Andy's supervisor as he was with his new roommate.

Dr. Dan tried unsuccessfully to suppress a smile. He glanced over at Andy and shrugged.

He's fantastic, she thought, as she watched him return one of Robbie's big, overgrown hugs. Then, tucking in Heather's blanket, he kissed her forehead gently. Bayshore Medical Center was very lucky to have someone as caring and as beautiful as Daniel Stewart on its staff. Of course Andy meant Dr. Dan was beautiful on the inside, a beautiful human being. But she wouldn't deny she found him beautiful on the outside, too.

"Andrea!" Mrs. Grymes's gruff supervisor voice shattered the fantasy Andy was forming about the very appealing doctor.

"Yes, Mrs. Grymes? I was just—"

"Wool-gathering while Dr. Stewart does your job? If you're all through here, perhaps we can find something a little more useful for you to do with your hands—besides spinning daydreams."

"Yes, Mrs. Grymes." Andy slowly inched toward the open door. Her N.I.T. supervisor seemed to wear a permanent disapproving look.

"I'm sure if you just try using your NIT-wits, Andrea, you can figure out somewhere you might make yourself a bit more useful. I can't keep this entire pediatric floor on schedule all by myself, now can I? That is why we have nurses-in-training, now, isn't it?" The last part of Mrs. Grymes's tirade was muffled, more to herself than out loud. Andy wasn't sure if she was expected to answer her supervisor's questions or not. She decided not to.

"Actually, I was just leaving, ma'am," she said softly.

"Would you please ask Joe to bring in his cart on your way out, Andréa?" asked Dr. Dan.

"Already on my way, Doc," called Joe from the doorway, where he'd been leaning and listening. "But thanks anyway, Handy Andy," he teased, as she pushed past him into the corridor.

"Very funny, Mr. Duffy," she sneered at him under her breath.

"My, my. Still feeling a wee bit prickly, are we?" Joe's eyes sparkled, and his nose crinkled up with glee as he teased her.

"*We* are not. You're the prickly one, with all your needles." Her voice shook with anger as she shot back her retort.

"And do I love to needle you, Handy Andy. It makes your lovely emerald eyes flash with green Irish fire."

"For your information, I don't happen to be Irish. So you can save the blarney. You just *stick* to your Dracula cart, Joe Duffy—and leave me alone!" Oh, why did she let him infuriate her like this? She wanted to stamp her feet and yell, both at the same time.

Joe gave a low, sinister-sounding laugh. *"I vill get you in my power yet, Andréa."* His even, white teeth seemed to grow into sharp, menacing fangs as he leaned over to whisper her name into her neck.

Andy was suddenly very much aware of Robbie's and Heather's gleeful shouts and loud clapping.

"Do the scary monster again, Joe," cheered Heather.

"Be Drakala. Be Drakala," begged Robbie.

Dr. Dan stared at her and Joe, an amused, if not somewhat incredulous smile on his lips. Mrs. Grymes glared at the two of them hotly and steamed. Once again Andy was blushing a vivid shade of red because of Joe Duffy's warped sense of humor and his unmerciful teasing. She'd never forgive him for today. Never!

"Will you please leave me alone?" she hissed through clenched teeth.

"For now. *But ve vill meet again, sveet Handy Andy,*" he warned.

"Never! Not if I can help it," she promised.

"Duffy! On the double," shouted Mrs. Grymes in her best sergeant's tone of voice.

Andy wondered if she'd heard their verbal exchange.

"Andrea! Wait for me there."

7

Andy knew Mrs. Grymes had heard them, and she felt her knees beginning to wobble.

"Coming," Joe answered too sweetly. He quickly pushed his cart into the room. "Duffy's Dracula Wagon at your service. *I've come to take your blood.*" He did a very realistic impression of Bela Lugosi.

"Me first. Me first," cried Robbie exuberantly. "I wanna give Drakala my blood."

"Then me," declared Heather bravely, her pale blue eyes wide. "Me and Robbie are going to give Drakala our blood. Huh, Robbie?" She didn't seem nearly as convinced as Robbie that it was such a good idea.

"Okay, you two. Dracula Joe will give each of you a turn," laughed Dr. Dan. "It beats me how you do it, Joe. You make the most outrageous jokes about taking samples of their blood, and the children love it. They can't wait for Duffy's Dracula Wagon to show up. They're better for you than for any other phlebotomist we have. I've seen adults act like bigger babies when they have to give blood."

"Must be my marvelous personality, Doc," bragged Joe.

"That must be it," laughed the doctor warmly.

"Hmph," snorted Mrs. Grymes at his joking boast. "If you can spare us, Doctor? Andrea and I have more important things to do than to stand here and listen to Mr. Duffy pat himself on the back."

For the first time Andy was glad Mrs. Grymes was such a let's-have-none-of-that-nonsense kind of person.

"Of course, Mrs. Grymes. You and Andréa go along."

"Andrea," called the N.I.T. supervisor, bustling off down the hall without even checking to see if she actually had Andy in tow.

Oh-oh, Andy thought in dread, here it comes. She had to march in double time to keep step with her N.I.T. troop leader. She knew without a doubt she was in for Mrs. Grymes's lecture on the Appropriate Behavior for a Nurse-in-Training. Not to mention numerous reminders to use her NIT-wits more often.

Following her supervisor to the next ward where beds awaited stripping and remaking, Andy remembered the day she'd met Joe

Duffy. It was her first day on the pediatric floor. She'd noticed him immediately. With his sky blue eyes and unruly mass of shining black hair, he was one of the best-looking guys in pediatrics. She'd watched him in his white lab coat, about six feet tall and kind of cute—for a boy phlebotomist—pushing his lab cart down the hall. He'd stopped to talk, and he'd told her how he planned to be a doctor of pediatrics one day. He'd seemed nice, and she'd liked her first impressions of Mr. Joe Duffy. But that was before Mrs. Grymes introduced her to Dr. Daniel Stewart, the head of pediatrics. After that, Joe Duffy, the boy phlebotomist, never entered Andy's thoughts again. Unless, like today, he did something to completely enrage her.

Andy carried a pile of dirty sheets into the hall. She went to the laundry cart and dropped them on top, staring down at the full canvas bin of soiled linens. She'd let Joe make her look foolish and inept. Never again, she told herself. Never, never, never again! Forget about him. There is no Joe Duffy. With a vengeance, Andy kept shoving the soiled laundry into the already overflowing cart.

What Are Friends For?

"MY FEET ARE the only alarm clock I need to tell me when it's quitting time," moaned Andy, stepping quickly into the elevator just as the doors were beginning to close.

"My feet stopped ticking about three this afternoon, when my battery went dead," sighed Andy's friend, Jackee. She was already in the elevator when Andy got on at pediatrics.

"An eight hour day, even in what Grymes calls 'sensible shoes,' can practically demolish two once totally perfect feet. I know I don't have one more step left in mine." Andy looked down at the two culprits and shook her head sadly.

"Tell me about it. If Monica's late tonight, I'm going to strangle her with my very own, very chapped bare hands," Jackee threatened. Monica was Jackee's roommate and another of Andy's good friends. All three girls were third-year student nurses in Bayshore University's Nurse-In-Training work-study program.

Andy felt the elevator's stop in the pit of her stomach. The doors slid open, and she and Jackee trudged side by side across the beige-carpeted hospital lobby; past the clusters of navy blue chairs and rust plaid couches, huddled together in groups like the people who waited on them, as if to offer shelter and protection; past the beautiful plants placed near the furniture and meant to give the waiting area a feeling of restfulness and tranquillity. The lights that had been turned up with the approach of evening glared uncomfortably into Andy's overtired eyes. She looked at the people who filled the lobby: some waited; others watched or wandered; some just worried. She was glad to be going home.

In one corner a tired-looking woman tried unsuccessfully to read to three overactive children. Two people sat on the edge of their seats as if they were waiting for a phone to ring. One man seemed frozen and stared straight ahead, while another couldn't sit still at all and endlessly paced the carpeted floor.

Andy often thought how pain and illness and love made equals of so many people who seemed to share nothing except their humanity.

She followed Jackee through the automatic double glass doors and under the portico of the hospital's front entrance. They headed across the parking lot toward a yellow VW Bug, Jackee's pride and joy. Looking back at the hospital, Andy was moved by the importance of the imposing ten-story building in which she worked. People often admired the unusual architecture of the hospital's stately curved facade. It was so much more than just a beautiful building. Bayshore Medical Center was one of the most modern, best staffed, and most caring medical facilities in Southern California. She was proud to be a part of its healing process.

But tonight her pride was tempered by tired feet. "I hope Monica gets here soon," she sighed.

"Monica Ross? Leave work on time? Not likely. She gets so involved with her babies and their new mamas, she forgets to come off duty. Dedication to one's work is admirable, but. . . ."

"Come on, Jack. We've waited for you too. Plenty of times."

"Moi?" Jackee's eyes opened wide in mock surprise.

Andy nodded her head decisively. "Yes, you. How about two weeks ago when you were late four nights in a row? Tucking in Mrs. Moiseeff after her cataract operation? And then there was two nights ago. Or have you forgotten, 'Just one more chapter,' for nice Mr. Gregory who had gallstones? You're as bad as Monica, Jack. Only with you, it's geriatric patients instead of maternity."

"Maybe. But then, so are you."

"Me too. I admit it." All of their N.I.T. friends were the same.

"We're all guilty—if you can be guilty—of caring too much."
The concerned look in Jackee's eyes faded; she was smiling again.

"But Monica does have a special thing for helpless little creatures, doesn't she?" Andy's question was more a statement of fact.

"Oh, tell me about that," Jackee groaned. "Every stray cat, mouse, lizard, frog, ladybug, and tarantula in town has lived, is living, or will live in our apartment. We've got more nonpaying guests than freebie night at the Y. Our apartment has been declared the second largest zoo in Los Angeles—and a public health hazard. I'm afraid to walk across my own floor barefoot. I have a sneaking suspicion my roommate is really Dr. Doolittle—not Nurse Ross."

Andy could barely walk straight, she was laughing so hard. It was all true. No matter what it was, if it needed a home and if Monica found it, Jackee wound up living with it.

"Okay, you two. What kept you, and what's so funny?" demanded Monica. She was leaning against Jackee's VW, tapping her foot.

"You, and the Y," giggled Jackee.

Monica shook her head. Pushing a straying strand of short-blonde hair out of her eyes, she stared up at her roommate. "You know what, Jack? Your license plate suits you perfectly: MSBUGGY! You are Ms. Buggy. A lot buggy-er than you know."

"And catty-er, and mousey-er, and froggy-er," roared Jackee. Her strawberry blonde frizz sprang to life as she laughed. Tiny corkscrew curls quivered and danced, escaping the flyaway topknot she wore, adding three more inches to her five feet seven.

"And don't forget tarantulay-er," chortled Andy. Even though she couldn't pronounce the tongue twister, she was sure Jackee knew what she meant.

"Don't bother to tell me what you two are so hysterical about," said Monica. "I'm too tired to laugh at it anyway."

"Sorry," murmured Jackee, overplaying her contrition. "Here we are wasting time, and for once—you're early."

"If that was meant to be a cleverly phrased accusation, I agree completely. I'm too beat to defend myself. Just unlock the door to this yellow garbage can on wheels, and let's go home."

12

"Monica's right, Jack. It's awful. What *is* all this junk?" Andy looked at the heap on the back seat of the small car.

"*Junk!* That is not junk. That's my wet suit, my weight belt, two sets of fins, a three-pronged spear, and my scuba tanks. That happens to be very professional, highly technological stuff back there. I need all that gear when I dive," announced Jackee indignantly.

"And Ms. Buggy doubles as a diving bell," teased Monica.

"Oh, yeah? Well, I'm very impressed, but where do I sit?" puzzled Andy.

"Just shove all that junk into the corner and crawl in," laughed Jackee. She held the seat up so Andy could move her scuba gear and get in.

"And she does mean crawl," warned Monica. "I'm sorry you're elected. It's the hips; I'd never get 'em out once I got 'em in. Everything Jackee owns is packed into that back seat."

"I have to keep all my worldly belongings in Ms. Buggy. Don't I, Andy? Our apartment's all filled up with creatures. Would you believe she tried to make a home for her mouse, Clyde, in my underwear drawer?"

"Monica Ross, your passion to adopt every homeless waif in the world is driving me—and my bug—buggy!" proclaimed Jackee.

"Isn't Jack cute when she gets irrational?" joked Monica. She turned to Andy in the back seat and rolled her blue-green eyes at her roommate. "That's why we let her live with us. She's so entertaining. The animals love her." Monica gave Jackee a huge gotcha grin.

Monica's good-natured teasing made Jackee laugh. Andy knew they were closer than friends, like sisters, and perfect together.

Starting the car, Jackee ground the gears into first, and they rabbit-hopped out of the parking lot.

The ride to Andy's house was not a long one. Taking the bus back and forth to the university, which she usually did, took twice as much time as driving. Tonight the ride was just long enough for the overtired threesome to become hysterical with laughter several times over. The extent of their fatigue magnified the silliness of their conversations. Even the not-so-funny Mrs. Grymes became a new source of amusement for Andy to share with her friends. But when

Monica and Jackee broke up with riotous laughter over her run-in with Joe Duffy, Andy was hard pressed to see what they found so funny. She'd been looking for some sympathy, or at least their serious agreement that his behavior had been totally impossible. Instead, Monica called him adorable, and Jackee decided Andy should get to know him better—if only to introduce him to her. Andy was disappointed in both of them. Their humorous attitude toward her compromising situation, which was all Joe Duffy's fault, wasn't funny! But she decided to forgive them; they hadn't met him yet.

By the time Jackee pulled the car to the curb in front of the two-bedroom, white stucco and red tile Santa Monica home where Andy lived with her dad, Lieutenant Andrew Whitman, the girls were all laughed out. Andy felt limp. It was a real struggle to scramble over the scuba gear and squeeze out of the tight back seat. Finally extracting her left foot from the trap of Monica's seat belt, she thanked Jackee for the fun company and the ride home.

Even with the silver gleam of the old-fashioned street lamp to light the pathway from the sidewalk to her house, Andy had to walk slowly to avoid the many fissures and cracks the years of ground shifting had produced. When you've lived in sunny Southern California your whole life, you accept buckled cement walkways and jiggling earth tremors as the bonus you get with the mortgage on your house. Andy had lived in the little house on Fourteenth Street all her life. Each hairline crack in the old concrete path represented another year of her growing up, and all the memories that went with it. One of those memories, a mixture of happy and sad, came to Andy's mind—her mom. The death of her mom had made the worst crack of all—in her heart, and in her life. And it left a huge empty spot in the house she and Big Andy called home.

With a heavy sigh she climbed the Spanish tile steps, pushed open the wrought-iron gate, and crossed the small patio to her front door. I'm just tired, she thought, suddenly feeling blue. She hesitated a moment before going in. She couldn't let her dad see her looking so down. She found her smile and put it on.

"Dad, I'm home," she called brightly, stepping into the dimly lit entryway just as Big Andy came out of the kitchen.

"Hi, honey." He looked at his watch. "Home a few minutes early, aren't you?" The broad shoulders of his six-foot-one body filled the narrow hall.

"A little. I got a ride home with Jackee and Monica; I didn't have to take the bus tonight."

"And how are two of my favorite NIT-wits getting along?"

"All of us N.I.T.s are absolutely terrific, of course."

"Oh, of course you are," he agreed, but Andy wasn't exactly sure how he meant that. "Tell me about your day while I get into my jacket. I was just leaving for headquarters. We've got a lead on that creep, the one the newspapers call the Venice rapist. I know I promised you a hot game of chess, honey. But. . . ."

"I'm glad my dad is the head of detectives for the LAPD."

"LAPD, Venice Division," added Big Andy.

"All I know is, with my very own father in charge of the task force that's after that guy, he doesn't stand a chance. Do you know how safe that makes me feel?"

"How safe?"

Andy slipped her arms around her dad's waist, and he gave her a hug. "About as safe as a little girl in her daddy's arms can feel. That's how."

Her dad hugged her tight. "But I've still got a few minutes to hear how my little girl's day went."

"I'm not really so little, am I? In some circles I'd be considered a grown woman."

"Not in mine." He hugged her again.

"But in no time at all, I'll be a graduated, full-fledged nurse," she said, holding up his jacket so he could slip in his long arms.

He tapped the end of her slightly freckled nose with his index finger. "I wish you weren't in such a big hurry, kiddo. First a woman, then a nurse. Before you know it, a wife and a mother. You'll be leaving your old dad too soon." Big Andy ran a huge, bear-paw hand through his thick salt and pepper hair. He smiled down at his daughter with sad hazel eyes. To Andy he was more like a lost little boy than the head of detectives, LAPD, Venice Division.

"I'm not going anywhere, Daddy. Not for a long time."

15

Because he wanted to hear all about the hours she wasn't with him, she began a humorous account of her day. Andy knew just how much her dad counted on her sharing her life with him. Andy knew he liked to feel he was a part of it, too. He was lonely. Big Andy missed his beloved wife Louise, Andy's mom, maybe even more than she did.

Andrew Whitman and Louise Charlotte Galee had been sweethearts in high school. At seventeen he'd sworn he'd never love anyone but her, or even look at another girl. In all their happy years of marriage, her mom had confided, he never did. Throughout Louise Whitman's long struggle with the cancer that finally overcame her, Big Andy had been beside her, holding her hand and loving her. And in the four years since his wife's death, he'd made his daughter's happiness the most important thing in his life.

For that reason, Andy usually related only those things about her classes and her N.I.T. work she knew would cheer him and give him pleasure. That's why she purposely omitted her confrontation with Joe Duffy and the displeasure their conflict had aroused in Mrs. Grymes. She did tell him about the fantastic Dr. Dan, but left out the part where he had to help her up off the floor. She went into great detail over Robbie Washington's near escape and her ride home in Jackee's Volkswagen. Her bout with the scuba gear made her dad chuckle.

"Sounds like you had a fun-filled day, honey," he teased.

"Fun? It sounded like fun to you? Oh, sure. Nursing is full of laughs," she retorted good-naturedly. "Remind me to tell you some good bedpan stories sometime."

"You know you love it."

"You're right; I do." She stretched up on her tiptoes to kiss his cheek. "But not nearly as much as I love you."

He grabbed her in another bear hug, then held her away from him and smiled. "Or I love you, kiddo. Your mother would be proud to know how well you're doing. While she was so sick, all the time you were taking care of her . . . before she died . . . you were the only one who could really comfort her. She said that you were better for her than pain pills, that you had the hands of an angel and the heart

16

of a saint. We both knew you were making the right choice when you decided to become a nurse.''

Andy knew those words hadn't come easily for her dad. They must bring back so many painful memories for him; she'd heard the catch in his voice as he spoke about her mom. But he was talking about her more and more. Andy thought that was a good sign. For a very long time, he wouldn't or couldn't speak about her at all.

"Hey, have you eaten anything, Dad? I don't want you to have any excuse for filling up on candy from a vending machine. Candy and instant coffee is no substitute for dinner.''

"Hot soup and cold spaghetti, you old mother hen. Now, lock the door behind me,'' he ordered, and kissed her good-bye.

Andy locked the door. Then, gathering up the books, purse, and sweater she'd dropped on the entryway table when she came in, she went into the kitchen. She studied the contents of the fridge for something to make for her own dinner. She lifted a few unpromising lids, shifted several uninteresting bottles and jars, wrinkled her nose, and settled for hot soup and cold spaghetti, too. Within minutes her meal was ready. She sat at the kitchen table she'd painted a bright "good morning" orange to match the new "good heavens" (as her dad had named it) yellow and orange wallpaper that she'd hung by herself. Slowly, slurping her chicken noodle soup, she thumbed through her class notes.

She was lost in concentration over an anatomy assignment, somewhere between the ulna and the femur, when the phone jangled, startling her.

"Hello," she said gaily into the receiver. She hated it when people answered the phone sounding as tired as she felt.

"Hello yourself," replied the caller in an equally cheerful voice.

"Liz! What's up?" Andy asked her friend. Like herself, Elizabeth Jones was a student nurse at Bayshore Medical.

"Not too much. May I ask you a question?"

"Lizzie, love, you may ask me anything—as long as it's not about ulnas and femurs.''

"Then it's been nice talking to you. See you tomorrow," Liz replied too quickly.

"Hey! Come on. I was only kidding. You having trouble with your anatomy, too?"

"Let me put it to you this way, honey. My legs could be a tad shorter, and my bottom a smidge smaller, but all in all, I can't complain." Both girls laughed.

Complain? Andy couldn't think of one thing about Liz that needed changing. She had the kind of body that ordinary girls would kill for: model tall and all perfectly symmetrically proportioned. Add to that the most spellbinding huge brown eyes, a very short (and very exotic) cap of jet black ringlets, and flawless skin the color of café au lait. Monica was bouncy and cute; Jackee was attractive and different; Gabby was small and pretty; and Sam was lovely and elegant; but Elizabeth Jones was gorgeous—too beautiful to describe. Everybody knew it, but Liz was just too unconceited to care.

"Will you be serious?" said Andy.

"Okay. Seriously, my problem is—I lost the paper I wrote our anatomy assignment on. I knew you'd have it."

"Read chapter eleven and do assignments one through seven in the workbook," Andy explained. "And good luck!"

"That bad, huh? Thanks anyway. Now I'm going to do you a favor," said Liz.

"That's nice. I hope?"

"Better than nice. I'm having a party on the Cookie Sunday afternoon. Can you come?"

"Another one?"

"Andy, child. Party nurse is a specialized field—almost as important to a hospital as its chief neurosurgeon. It is an area of medicine for which I am ably qualified. As nurses, our job is to help people get well. Parties create happiness, and they make people feel better. One cannot have too much happiness or too many parties in one's life. Can one?"

"Not if one lives on a sailboat tied to a rusty old dock, and can't afford the price of a cup of coffee, one can't," joked Andy. A picture of the huge sailboat on which Liz lived, the Chocolate Ship Cookie, appeared in her mind. It was worth a small fortune, and that's exactly what it cost to keep it anchored at the exclusive Sea

Cove Landing in glorious Bayshore Marina. If Liz wasn't such a sweet person and such a good friend, Andy decided, she'd be easy to hate. But, like everyone else who knew her, Andy loved her.

"Does that mean you'll come?"

"Can I let you know tomorrow? Mrs. Grymes asked if I wanted to work as an aide on Sunday, and I told her yes. If she doesn't need me, I'd love to come."

"Try. And bring a date."

"A date?"

"Sure. If you want to. I've already spoken to Monica and Jackee. They're going to bring two guys Jack knows from geriatrics."

"Both over eighty," laughed Andy.

"Probably," giggled Liz. "I called Gabby, too. She'd already volunteered to woman the dawn patrol at the clinic for the Crisis Unit. If she can still stand up when she gets off duty, she'll ask her brother Tonio to drop her off at the boat. Jack said she'd take her home if Tonio doesn't want to stay."

"How many people have you invited, besides the gang?" In her mind, Andy could see the Cookie sinking into the sea.

"About a million—give or take a hundred. All guys!"

"Just the usual, huh? Sounds great. I'll do my best."

"Oh. Can I ask you one more thing? Will you call Sam and tell her about the party? Her aristocratic grandmother, Mrs. Crane, doesn't like me very much. She really lets Sam have it when I call there. I would venture to say that black is not one of her favorite colors. She acts as if Sam will get contaminated."

"Oh, no, Liz. You have to be mistaken, in this day and age. How can you think Sam is prejudiced?"

"Not Sam. Her snob hill, too too grand mama. The old battle-ax has hung up on me several times. Sam said she swore it was the phone's fault we were disconnected. But even Sam felt the only thing disconnected was dear Mrs. Crane's good manners."

"I hate to believe you're right. But of course I'll call Sam for you. I'll have her call back. And thanks again for asking me."

"Remember, bring a date—for sure."

19

"Like who?" There was no one she was dating. No one she wanted to ask.

"Like anyone. I don't care. Who would you like to ask?"

"Dr. Dan," Andy blurted. Suddenly she realized what she'd said. A truth she hadn't even admitted to herself.

"Daniel Stewart? Dr. Pediatrics? Girl, are you crazy? Have you joined his ga-ga club too? Not you, Andy?"

"Why not? I think he's fantastic."

"Every woman at Bayshore thinks he's fantastic—even his wife."

"I know," whispered Andy. "I know."

"Besides, that man's too old for you. He's practically forty. You're thinking dumb. Married doctors are no-no's."

"He isn't forty. He's thirty-nine. And I know it's dumb. It was just wishful thinking, Liz. Don't worry."

"Forget the good doctor. What about that cute hunk, Joe Duffy, from the lab?"

"What about him?"

"Now that's someone I could see you taking an interest in. Joe Duffy makes sense for you."

"Joe Duffy doesn't make anything for me—but trouble!"

"He's adorable."

"He's a pest."

"He's sweet."

"He's a goof."

"He's perfectly gorgeous, Andrea Leigh Whitman!"

"And you're perfectly nuts, Elizabeth Lucrezia Jones. But I forgive you."

"Only because I'm right, and you know it. You just need some of sister Liz's friendly advice. Isn't that what friends are for? Call Sam for me. Don't forget."

"I'll call. Right this minute—if you hang up. Friend!"

"I'm hanging. And think about Joe Duffy," Liz urged.

"Not if I can help it," promised Andy, hanging up the receiver.

20

3

Proposals, Problems, Peter Pan

THERE'S NO PLACE in the world I'd rather live than in Santa Monica, thought Andy, as she turned the corner from quiet, residential Fourteenth Street onto bustling Montana Avenue. Rain or shine, her brisk morning walks to the bus stop always brought her a special sense of pleasure. Montana Avenue was a lovely step backward in time to an old-fashioned way of life, a time when people lived in neighborhoods, and they smiled at one another, and they knew each other's names. Andy's favorite street was her own friendly island in a sea of impersonal, multistoried, neon-lit shopping malls, peopled with wandering strangers. She loved to stroll along the busy avenue under the ancient mulberry trees; she couldn't think of a thing she enjoyed more. Their green foliage shaded the colorful and enticing window displays in the shops lining both sides of the street. And almost every one of the small stores was owned by an old friend. The merchants, like the cracks in her sidewalk, were a part of Andy's growing up. She eagerly returned all the shopkeepers' waves and friendly good mornings.

As she neared Mr. Pakkala's bakery, she prepared herself to resist the delicious and tempting aromas that would soon assault her nose, her taste buds, and her sense of N.I.T. duty.

"Good morning, Mr. Pakkala. You smell wonderful, as usual," called Andy to the little man in the oversized white apron who, as he did every morning, attempted to lure her inside his shop by arranging freshly baked breads and pastries in his window.

"Good morning to you, Nurse Andy. Come in. Come have a cup of tea with me, with maybe one little croissant? Come, before the bus. Come. Come," pleaded Mr. Pakkala, waving her inside.

Of all the merchants on Montana Avenue, Andy had known Mr. Pakkala the longest. He was like her special adopted uncle.

"I wish I could. Just passing your doorway always makes my mouth water. But today I can't. I have a full day's duty at the hospital, and if I don't catch the next bus, I'll be late."

As they talked, the chubby baker threw up his hands. He began putting some of his flaky, buttery croissants into a bag. Then he waddled to the open door and handed the bag to Andy.

"These are for you and your nice nursie friends at the hospital. How can I let you start the day without one of Mr. Pakkala's special croissants?"

Andy reached inside her purse.

"No, no. From Mr. Pakkala to his favorite little nurse. So, no money; on me. Now, go save lives—but don't work too hard." His dark eyes gleamed at her over his bulbous nose and thick black mustache.

"But Mr. Pakkala, I couldn't."

"What is couldn't? Of course you can. I can give a gift to my own little Andy, can't I? Now you better run—or that big blue bus is going to arrive at your Bayshore Medical Center one nursie short."

"Oh, no!" Andy saw the bus pull up to her stop. The several people who'd been waiting began to board. "Thank you for the treat, Mr. Pakkala. I know the girls will love it," she shouted over her shoulder, as she dashed to the corner. The bus doors hissed closed just as she reached them.

"Jim, Jim," she yelled, banging on the closed doors and waving her bag of croissants frantically at the driver. The sealed doors miraculously hissed open again.

"Almost missed you this time, Miss Whitman." Jim smiled warmly.

"Almost," gasped Andy. "Thank you, Jim." She fished in her purse until she found the change to drop in the money box. Slowly the bus pulled away from the curb. Andy clutched her croissants and her purse in the same hand. She used her free hand to grab at the poles as she swayed down the aisle to find a seat.

"What if I move over so you can sit with me?" asked an unpleasantly familiar voice. It came from the newspaper before her. The bus made a sudden lurch, and she had to grab the seat rail to keep from falling into the open newspaper. Slowly the paper was lowered, and the dreaded face behind it grinned up at her. She was trapped by crystal clear blue eyes, twinkling merrily at her.

"What if you don't move, Joe Duffy." She knew she was being very rude, but she couldn't stop herself. His stare unnerved her. She quickly took a seat behind him, next to a kindly looking old lady. The woman appeared to be harmless; she seemed to be asleep. But that didn't matter. Confronted with the choice of sitting next to either Joe Duffy or Godzilla, she'd have picked Godzilla any day!

"Your friend is waving at you, dear," said her seatmate in a hushed voice. The old woman looked at her through half-closed eyes, magnified many times over by her thick glasses. She wasn't asleep after all.

"Thank you, but he's not my friend," Andy told her. She stared out the window without seeing anything.

"It's true; we're more than friends. I'm her fiancé, but we've had a lovers' quarrel. We were to marry in one week; now she won't even speak to me."

Andy's head jerked around, and she glared at him. Of all the—

"Oh, my," said the old woman, shaking her head at Andy. She looked at Joe sympathetically.

How dare he say that? He won't get away with it. I won't let him. "We are *not* getting married at all. See? No ring." Andy held out her left hand for the woman to check. "No ring!" She was talking loud enough for the whole bus to hear. Well, let them. She was too indignant to care. Just what did Mr. Duffy think he was doing, anyway?

"What did I tell you? She won't marry me—and just because I can't afford to buy her a ring." With a sigh he rested his chin on the back of the seat, looking absolutely pathetic.

This act was even worse than his Dracula routine.

"Dear me! You poor boy." The sweet, understanding lady patted Joe's hand and tried to console him. She glared with great, magnified eyes at Andy, her mouth pursed disapprovingly.

"Please. We only work together. I hardly know him." Again, Andy tried to defend herself against Joe's accusations.

"We work at the medical center," Joe said. "I'm only in the lab now. That's why I can't afford to buy her a ring. But, when I'm a famous doctor, I've promised to make it up to her. I'll buy her diamonds, emeralds to match her eyes, a new silver sheriff's badge, anything." The sincerity of his face pleaded his case.

Not since she was ten years old and tangled with Alex Purcellini on the school playground had Andy wanted to punch someone as much as she did now.

This was too much. The old woman patted Joe's cheek. She smoothed his hair. At Andy she clicked her tongue. Andy picked up her purse and the croissant bag from her lap. She left her seat and went to stand near the rear door of the bus. She knew that every passenger on the bus had heard the terrible things that Joe had said. And now, they were staring at her in amusement. It wasn't funny. She kept her eyes focused on the two small windows in the back door of the bus.

They were almost to the hospital. She could see the boats at Sea Cove Landing. Today the ocean looked as angry and upset as she felt. Wind ruffled the waves, sending whitecaps against the tossing boats. The bus stopped at the Bayshore Marina. The next stop would be hers—and Joe's.

She refused to think about him; he was probably staring at her back this very minute. She concentrated on the marina scenery instead.

Look at the beautiful redwood town houses and the Cape Cod–

24

style condominiums, she told herself. See the lovely rainbow-colored sails on the boats bobbing up and down at their private docks. Don't think about him! She tried not to. It was all a blur as the bus sped toward her stop. Finally, she saw the university. The ivy-covered stone and brick buildings meant that they were crossing the campus at last and would be stopping at the Bayshore Medical Center in a very few minutes.

At the squeal of the bus's brakes, the doors sprung open. Tightening her grip on her croissant bag and purse, she ran for the hospital. She heard Joe calling her name. He was laughing. Telling her it was just a joke. Asking her to let him apologize. Begging her to wait for him. But she wouldn't stop. She never wanted Joe Duffy to speak to her again. He had nothing to say she wanted to hear.

"You look a bit flushed; don't you feel well?" Mrs. Grymes asked Andy. "We do need every nurse we have in pediatrics. Still, you know how dangerous it is to come to work if you're coming down with something." The supervisor delivered her message with a stern and unsmiling face.

Andy doubted it was *her* health her supervisor was actually concerned with. Good ol' Grymes, she thought. I could collapse in a dead faint, and she'd have someone disinfecting the tiles before I hit the floor. Probably me! "No, ma'am, I'm not ill. But thank you for your concern." Andy's skeptical statement of gratitude brought a smile (or was it a smirk?) to Mrs. Grymes's face. "I was running from the bus. I didn't want to be late reporting for duty."

"Yes. Well, catch your breath. Then start your rounds in four. Robbie Washington's been asking for you all morning. And remember, Andrea. . . . NIT-wits. Use your NIT-wits."

"Yes, Mrs. Grymes. I'll remember. Thank you." Andy watched her supervisor disappear into the waiting elevator car. She shook her head; what a morning she'd had already. She'd just faced the Mrs. Grymes Health Check and NIT-wit Reminder Session—without a giggle. She'd survived a Joe Duffy. She felt prepared to brave anything. Her self-confidence was restored. She felt as calm she had when her day began, when she'd talked with Mr. Pakkala. Her tummy growled. Suddenly she was very hungry for one of his delicious croissants. Her stomach had been in such a turmoil when she first arrived that she didn't think she could keep down a rich French roll. She'd left them in the lounge for the other nurses. Now she hoped there would be one left for her when she was able to take her break.

"Okay, Robbie, you little bandit," Andy sang out softly as she started for room four. "I'm ready for you, today. And you had better not try any of that funny stuff on ol' Sheriff Andy, here." *Sheriff?* She hadn't meant to say that. She felt like kicking herself.

" 'Morning, kids," she said cheerfully.

"Hi ya, Andy. Where ya been?" asked Robbie.

"Home. I do go home at night."

"You don't sleep here?" he questioned.

"No, I don't. I live in a house in Santa Monica with my dad," she explained. She checked his water pitcher and plumped his back pillows.

"Hey, me too."

"You live in Santa Monica with my dad?" teased Andy. "I wonder why I never noticed you?"

"No, that's silly. I live in Santa Monica with my mama and papa and Marcus, my big brother, and Edward M., my dog," said Robbie. "Does Dr. Dan live at the hospital?"

"Nope."

"Mrs. Grymes?"

"No, she has a home, too. Why so many questions?"

"She didn't go home last night," he confided.

"She didn't? Why do you say that, Robbie?" asked Andy.

"Cuz I saw her sit with Heather in the night. It got real late. I couldn't see any more television, and all the lights were turned off. Heather was crying. Huh, Heather?"

It was then that Andy realized Heather hadn't spoken a single word to her since she'd entered the room. She went over to her bed.

"Heather?" she called softly. The child was buried under her covers. "Heather, honey? What's the matter?" Her only answer was the tearful shudder of a frightened child. "Come on, honey. Let

Andy hold you, and you tell me why you're crying." She lowered the metal side rail on the bed and sat down.

Slowly a shiny batch of blonde curls emerged, followed by misty blue eyes and tear-stained cheeks. Andy scooped Heather into her arms and held her close.

"Dr. Fricker is going to take away my tonsils today," sobbed Heather.

"You don't want those nasty old tonsils. The tonsils are making you feel sick. You'll feel good enough to go home after Dr. Fricker takes them away. Wouldn't you like that?"

"I don't have to go home. I don't want an op'ration. I don't want one."

"I promise you, Heather. The operation won't be as terrible as you think. We talked about it. Don't you remember?"

"I 'member." Heather hiccuped. "I go to sleep, and when I wake up, my tonsils are gone. . . . And I get ice cream."

Robbie was across his bed stretched out on his stomach. He listened intently to Heather describe her coming surgery. "Me too. I want to get ice cream for my operation," he announced.

"I'm afraid you're not going to have an operation, Robbie," Andy informed him.

"Can I have ice cream with Heather, anyways?" he asked hopefully.

"I think that can be arranged, young man. That is, providing you don't give Heather and me any more scares. No more getting out of bed alone. Okay? Promise?"

"Okay. Promise," he agreed eagerly.

"When your sick tonsils are gone, you're going to feel so much better, Heather. And I'll bet your mother will be here when you wake up, waiting to feed you ice cream." Andy realized she had seen very little of Mrs. Berk, Heather's mother. She wondered why.

"My mommy might not like to come. But I'll be good. I will." Without warning, Heather was crying again. The quivering child clutched at Andy's neck so tightly that she found it difficult to breathe. "Please, Andy. Please. I'll be good. I promise. I promise," she whimpered over and over.

27

"Shush. Shush, sweetheart. Don't cry," Andy implored her. "I know you will. You're always a good girl."

"You won't leave me, will you, Andy?" Heather's sobs were verging on the hysterical.

"Of course not. I'll stay with you as long as you want me to." Her promise to remain and her soothing hugs seemed to comfort the child a little.

Andy was extremely concerned over Heather's behavior. She seemed far more distraught than normal about her tonsillectomy. Perhaps that was because she thought her mother didn't like coming to the hospital. Andy was beginning to think it might be true.

As she hugged her and rubbed her back, whispering little endearments that turned Heather's whimpers into tiny, gasping sighs, Andy was surprised to discover several small, dark bruises on the little girl's upper arms. It looked as if someone had held her too tightly for too long. Andy's innermost thoughts were following a course that frightened her. And it didn't help when she remembered how out of proportion Heather's fear had seemed over yesterday's incident with Robbie. There had to be a reasonable explanation. Andy felt a cold chill settle in her heart; she prayed it wasn't what she suspected—and feared.

Before allowing her imagination to run away with her reason, she had to be sure. She had to talk to someone who knew about these things. Gabby! Her friend at the Crisis Center; she'd know what to do. Talk to Gabby and be sure—absolutely sure!

Satisfied that Heather was no longer upset and was back to her usual antics with Robbie, Andy promised to read them a story later on. Then she started out the door to finish her rounds. The annoying racket, as she left the room, of two children arguing over which story she should read—*Curious George* or *Peter Pan*—was music to her ears.

Ward five was not filled with music; it blared forth with total bedlam. As Andy pushed open the door, very loud, very unhospital-like laughter and shouting poured out to meet her. She wasn't surprised. This room held three of the older children in Andy's care. Even if she'd had six arms, twelve hands, and one hundred twenty fingers, these patients would be more than a handful.

Eric Yeager, who was bedridden and in traction for the two legs he'd broken in a fall while hiking with his parents, seemed to find his immobility an insignificant handicap. The paper airplanes he was lobbing at Jason Fox's head were right on target.

Jason was the same age as Eric, but that didn't seem to make the two eleven-year-olds friends. There always seemed to be some kind of friction between them for Andy to mediate. And today was no exception. Jason whirled around the room in his wheelchair threatening Eric with great bodily injury, if he could only get close enough to bean him with his crutch.

Andy took the crutch away from him.

In the middle of all this chaos, Albert Raymond Lai was jumping up and down on his bed, cheering both of the bigger boys on to victory. And, although Andy marveled at his sense of fair play, she knew how dangerous excitement and physical activity could be for Albert's asthma.

"Eric, Jason, that will be enough." Andy scooped Albert, who was small for his age, off his bed. "And you stop acting like a jumping bean, Mr. Lai, and show these two overgrown hoodlums how a young man of nine should behave." Albert giggled as she tucked him into his bed.

"Eric, you stupid meathead, I'm going to kill you," yelled a frustrated Jason, who'd replaced his more lethal crutch with a pillow he now swung in Eric's direction. Jason was a problem. The loss of his right leg, in the car crash that had killed his little brother, had forced him to make many adjustments in his life. Not all of his adjustments seemed to be going as well as learning to maneuver his wheelchair efficiently. Andy noticed that Jason often took out his anger and frustration in mean and aggressive actions.

But this time it appeared that Eric was as much to blame as Jason was. Andy felt Eric was teasing him on purpose.

"Both of you, stop," she demanded in her sternest nurse voice. "Jason, put that pillow back on your bed immediately. Now!"

29

Jason halted, his pillow poised in midair, a sinister gleam in his eyes.

"Now, Jason. And if. . . ." She was too late. A paper missile sped past Jason's head and hit her in the shoulder. "And if one more of these dangerous little things is thrown in this room, or—"

"But Jason—" Eric began in his own defense.

"Or if one more pillow is swung at anybody—I don't care why— the person doing the throwing or the swinging will be moved to another room. Understand?" She looked from one boy to the other.

They nodded silently.

Andy was fully aware, even with the seeming animosity between them, that Jason and Eric wanted to be together. Jason's excuses for staying in their room to fight with Eric, rather than go to the play patio without him, were flimsy at best. They needed each other to lean on; even if they didn't realize it, Andy did. Given time they'd become friends, she hoped—before they throttled one another.

Without comment, both boys had suddenly become very busy: Eric unfolding his supply of paper airplanes; Jason raising and lowering his bed with the control button.

"Everything in hand, Andrea?" asked Mrs. Grymes.

Andy spun around, feeling the color drain out of her cheeks. Where had she come from? How long had she been there? The look of her supervisor's face told her very little. Ready to brave anything, she reminded herself, smiling brightly at Mrs. Grymes.

"We're doing just fine, Mrs. Grymes. Aren't we, guys?" Even Albert nodded enthusiastically with the two older boys.

"You finish your rounds, Andrea; I'll just help Jason find the play patio. Don't you think that would be a good idea—Eric?" The silence that answered Mrs. Grymes's question was loud indeed.

Andy started to leave the room. She wasn't sure if her N.I.T. supervisor approved of her method of handling the confrontation between the two boys.

"Andrea?"

"Yes, Mrs. Grymes."

"That was using your NIT-wits."

"Thank you, Mrs. Grymes." Thank you, thank you, thank you.

30

Andy felt like skipping down the hall to the next ward, but that wasn't appropriate behavior for one of Mrs. Grymes's N.I.T.s.

Her rounds finished, Andy checked with her supervisor (who complimented her work once more) and said she would be in room four reading to Heather and Robbie. It was an enjoyable part of her usual daily routine that she always looked forward to.

"Here I am." When she entered their room, Andy was surprised to find Heather on her knees laughing gaily.

Joe Duffy's cart stood between the two beds, and Joe was busy looking over, under, and around the visitor's chair.

"Robbie's gone. Robbie's gone," squealed Heather.

Oh, no. Not again? I'm going to have to tie him in his bed, she decided.

"I know you're hiding in there somewhere. Yoo-hoo, Robbie? Where are you?" called Joe. He didn't seem very worried.

"Excuse me, *Mr.* Duffy. Is Robbie missing or not?" Andy didn't bother to disguise her irritation, and her tone of voice wasn't pleasant. Even to her own ears, she sounded like a close imitation of Mrs. Grymes.

"Missing. Absolutely. He's gone, all right, *Miss* Whitman." Joe put his finger to his lips to signal silence, then pointed to Robbie's bed and the wiggling lump in it. "Can't seem to find him anywhere."

No wonder he didn't sound concerned. He knew Robbie was under his blankets the entire time.

"Where could he be? Where could he be?" wondered Joe out loud. The bump in the bed giggled.

Heather screeched and clapped her hands. "I know. I know," she laughed.

"Hmm?" Joe muttered, slowly easing his way around Robbie's bed. *"Gotcha!"* he shouted triumphantly, pulling back the covers. "Thought you could fool me, did you?"

"Heather told. She said where I was," groused Robbie. "No fair."

"I never," denied Heather. "I did not."

"She did not," confirmed Andy.

"I don't need any help; I'm Sherlock Holmes," announced Joe.

"You're not Sirlock Home, Joe; you're Drakala," argued Robbie.

"You're right, Rob. And guess what I have to do now?"

"Get some blood, right?" said Robbie, sticking out his small thin arm.

"Okay?"

"Sure, Joe. It's okay." Robbie sounded a little more subdued as he gave Joe permission to take his blood.

Ignoring Joe as he joked, teased, and charmed Robbie, Andy turned to Heather. "Want me to read that story now?"

"Yes, please."

"Which story do you guys want to hear?"

"You can read *Peter Pan* for Heather, Andy. That's the one she likes the best," Robbie announced gallantly.

Joe was preparing to take Robbie's blood.

"What part are we on, Heather?" She thumbed through the book. She'd read it to the children so many times that all of it looked familiar.

"Read about Captain Hook and the crocodile," said Robbie.

"Yes," Heather agreed. "Where Wendy gets saved by Peter."

"I think Heather is a romantic," sighed Joe. "If Robbie here doesn't grab you up first, Heather, will you marry me?"

"I had the impression this morning that you were already engaged." Her words shot out angrily before Andy could stop them.

"I was. But the love of my life spurned me. I'm afraid I was jilted. And in front of a bus full of people, too. So—I'm available, if you're interested."

"Hmph!" snorted Andy, sorry she'd begun the conversation. What happened to the promise she'd made herself never to talk to Joe Duffy again? Why did he make her so mad?

She began to read, starting where Peter bravely swoops down to rescue Wendy from Captain Hook and his evil pirates. Soon she was so engrossed in the story, reading all the characters in make-believe voices, that she forgot about Joe Duffy.

"Enjoyed your story, Andy. Very much. You make an adorable Wendy. I'd play Peter Pan with you any day." Without waiting to hear her retort, he pushed his cart out of the room.

Peter Pan was the perfect part for him. Andy closed the book and stared at the picture of the boy who never grew up. Joe was a lot like Peter. He was brash, outspoken, always expecting to get his own way, the perpetual little boy. Andy smiled to herself. Joe Duffy shouldn't be too difficult for her to handle; she'd always had a way with children.

She put away the book and began straightening Robbie's and Heather's beds.

Maybe I have been a little too hard on him, she thought as she worked. Everyone else seems to like him. Just because I think he's a pest (and he was one, where she was concerned), that doesn't mean he isn't a good lab tech. Or that he wouldn't make a fine doctor. It's obvious that the children adore him. Maybe it's that pesky, little boy, Peter Pan quality in him that appeals to them so much. I have to admit he is the best phlebotomist on the floor. His work has always been above reproach; it's his teasing personality that grates. Of course, he'll never be a Dr. Dan. No one could. Even so, he could still be a wonderful pediatrician. As she mused and speculated over Joe Duffy's possible future, the tiny spark of an unanswered question nibbled at the back of her thoughts. Then the spark blazed into a flame. She stood holding Robbie's six-shooter, staring at it, without moving.

Why in the world was Joe Duffy on my bus this morning? He's never taken the bus with me before!

"Andrea! Remember . . . NIT-wits . . . not daydreaming. Report to ward seven."

"Right now, Mrs. Grymes." She put the toy gun, with the sheriff's badge stamped on the handle grip, down on the table.

It's funny, she thought as she rushed to seven. Joe sat so quietly and listened so intently while I read; I forgot he was even there. Was he trying to be nice? Or to apologize for this morning? Oh, well, she decided, he probably just loves *Peter Pan.*

4

Relying on NIT-wits

AND AFTER ALL I've done for them, thought Andy with an amused chuckle. She walked along the corridors peeking through the open doors into the children's rooms. It was visiting hours, and that was always a special time for her little charges—a time when a nurse wasn't usually needed, not even Nurse Andy. She really didn't mind. She could always use the free time to catch up on many of the more time-consuming and less nurselike chores she had to deal with—like taking inventory of the clean linen supply or making repairs to the play patio after the morning cyclone of kids had passed through it. Happy laughter and excited chatter floated out of the rooms from all the contented children who visited with eagerly awaited parents. She wasn't jealous of the generous outpouring of love the parents received from her patients. All children were wonderful, warm, and loving—but fickle—creatures too. All morning she'd been both their nurse and their mother. She'd loved "her children," and they'd loved her back. Now they only wanted the warm hugs and kisses their own real mommies and daddies could give. Still, inside, Andy actually enjoyed their fickleness. After the parents were gone, it would be her turn and that of the other nurses who cared for and comforted the children. She knew she'd get her share of squishy hugs and sloppy kisses, exchange many I-love-yous, and receive an abundance of tired, grateful smiles. Andy believed these were the bonuses that made nursing such a "well-paid" profession.

One look at the linen closet and Andy's worst suspicions were confirmed. It was impossible to tell the last time anyone had straightened it up. It looked as if it had been done weeks, maybe even months ago. Now it was a major disaster area. She turned on the light and bravely entered into the midst of the disorder. She remembered to leave the door ajar. She'd been told many times that it was imperative that all the nurses on duty remain available and within the sound of a page at all times, should they be needed. She took the clipboard, which held the inventory pad, from its hook and placed it on the shelf in front of her. As she straightened, folding and aligning the closet's contents, she made notes on what items were running low. After thirty minutes of tedious work, she felt she was finally making headway, when a loud commotion in the corridor disturbed her concentration.

"Someone help me! Oh, my Lord, it's my baby! Please, help me!"

Andy rushed from the closet and collided with the frantic Mrs. Washington. One look at the hysterical woman's face and she knew what had happened: Robbie was having another grand mal, an epileptic seizure, and Mrs. Washington was terrified for her child. Andy's first duty lay with Robbie, and she left the distraught mother for another nurse to calm. She dashed for room four.

Robbie was on the floor between his bed and Heather's. Andy was relieved to see that Heather was not in the room. She was positive that Robbie's seizure would have frightened the girl, and she couldn't comfort Heather and help Robbie too. The convulsions that whipped the small boy's body caused him to arch his back, flinging out his arms and legs simultaneously. Andy forgot her own fears for Robbie as her skill and training took over. She dropped to her knees beside him, pushing a nearby chair across the room with one violent shove. A split-second survey of the area surrounding the bed told her there were no dangerous objects within Robbie's reach. She eased her right hand beneath the boy's head and very carefully turned him toward her. The aerated saliva that foamed on his lips, and could

35

cause him to choke, began to drain from the side of his mouth. Robbie's thrashing prevented her from turning him completely on his side, but she pulled down a pillow from his bed and was able to slightly elevate his hips with it as she had been instructed to do. Without constricting his movements she tried to protect him from striking himself, or from a more serious injury, such as banging his head. Every movement she made was economical and unconsciously designed to help her reserve her strength, for her patient's benefit, until needed help arrived. Several times she made an effort to reach Robbie's emergency button on the wall behind the bed, only inches away from her fingers, but she couldn't touch the buzzer without releasing Robbie's head, which she needed to hold and keep turned toward her. As quickly as they appeared, the convulsions could also disappear. As Robbie's spasms began to ease, Andy reached for the emergency call button and rang it several times. Although once was enough to alert the nurses' station, Andy felt better making sure they'd heard her. She returned to the side of the exhausted child, now lying quietly on the floor, gathered him into her arms, and lifted him onto the cool, white sheets of his bed.

Not until that moment did she notice Mrs. Washington crying and twisting her hands together at the foot of her son's bed. Andy hadn't realized it, but Robbie's mother had followed her back into the room. She'd accepted Andy as all the help her little boy needed, not looking further for additional assistance. That knowledge gave Andy's pride a boost. She was pleased to be thought of as a competent nurse.

Suddenly the room was a beehive of efficient medical activity.

Mrs. Grymes stood beside Mrs. Washington, holding her hand. The head pediatric nurse, Mrs. Wernick, and several other very capable nurses were hovering about Robbie's bed assisting Dr. Dan.

Andy felt herself being pushed farther and farther back from Robbie's bedside. Now that the danger was over, she had time to think and feel again. She was surprised by the fierce pounding of her heart and the frenzied rushing of her blood, spurred on by her adrenaline. Robbie was in good hands now—the best—but Andy felt close to collapse. She couldn't even muster enough energy to feel surprised when Mrs. Grymes took her by the hand, her other arm around the quivering Mrs. Washington, and led them both away to the nurses' lounge.

Sitting on the old green couch next to Robbie's mother, Andy felt her pulse begin to slow and return to normal. She accepted the cup of coffee Mrs. Grymes held out to her, placing it on the low table next to the arm of the couch. She looked at her hands; they had almost stopped shaking. She'd reacted instinctively to Robbie's need, and now she was feeling the release of pent-up pressures from the past few very hectic minutes.

Mrs. Washington stared with faraway eyes at the cup the N.I.T. supervisor offered her. Andy took the cup of steaming coffee and held it up, trying to tempt Robbie's mother with the aroma.

"Try to drink a little of this, Mrs. Washington. Everything is going to be just fine now. Dr. Dan's with Robbie." Andy's words of comfort seemed to go unheard.

"You saved his life. You saved my Robbie. I don't know how to thank you, Miss Whitman. My baby might have died; you saved his life," repeated Mrs. Washington.

"Robbie wasn't going to die. You mustn't think that. His seizures aren't nearly as severe as they were when he entered Bayshore. You were just frightened," soothed Andy, calming herself by reassuring the teary-eyed mother.

"The doctor said the new medicine would stop the seizures. He promised. But it was worse this time. I know it was."

"Andrea's right, Mrs. Washington. It wasn't worse. It's just that Robbie has gone so long this time without an attack, you've forgotten." Mrs. Grymes took a seat in the big chair across from the couch. She sipped her coffee, but her eyes never wavered over the rim of her cup. "The doctors promised only that Robbie's epilepsy could be controlled. He's had longer and longer periods between the seizures. You know that."

"No. I know they said no more attacks—ever. I know it."

"What Dr. Dan did promise you and Robbie is hope. He said there was an excellent chance that once Robbie's seizures were under control, they might disappear altogether. He said *might*. And he did promise to do everything in his power to make that happen. But you must also remember that he said there were never any guarantees." Mrs. Grymes spoke kindly to Mrs. Washington, but realistically. Anything less would have been cruel.

Again Andy held the cup of coffee out to the distracted woman. This time she took it into her own hands and began to sip.

"I do know that. And Robbie has shown so much improvement. I was just frightened, Mrs. Grymes; you're right. He's so tiny, and he's been so sick. If only his father had been here. Robbie's grand mal seizures frighten me so. I've tried to be brave. I promised Will I would be brave—for Robbie, and for Marcus, his big brother. It's so hard when Will's away. It's not his fault that his company has him traveling so much of the time."

"I know," agreed Andy. She smiled at the way talking about her children seemed to make Mrs. Washington happy, revive her spirits, and calm her fears. "I'll bet Robbie is the spitting image of his daddy."

"Oh, he is. Well, at least I think so." Mrs. Washington was visibly more relaxed now. "But Will says no. He says Robbie looks just like me, because . . . I'm the pretty one; but it's not true. Both my boys are just like Will—handsome as the day is long. Robbie's practically Marcus's shadow, though. Why, he follows that boy everywhere and mimics all his mannerisms—even the bad ones." Mrs. Washington laughed and then recalled several cherished memories of her two rambunctious sons.

Andy and Mrs. Grymes joined her, chuckling lightly.

"That is until . . . the epilepsy started, before Robbie became so sick. Now . . . ?" Her brow wrinkled with worry once more.

"Now . . . Robbie will get better. And better. And better," said Dr. Dan, hearing the end of Mrs. Washington's statement as he entered the lounge.

The three woman turned to look at him as he walked toward them. His smile, directed at Mrs. Washington, was filled with compassion and optimism. "But right now," he continued, "I think you and I ought to have another little talk about what you should expect from Robbie's already much improved condition. And perhaps, just a few

38

more words, for reinforcement, about what you can do if he has a seizure while you're with him. Are you up to it?''

Mrs. Washington nodded. "Is he all right, Doctor? I have to go to him.'' She stood up, clutching the empty coffee cup tightly between tense hands.

"He's fine now. He's fallen asleep. And sleep is what he needs most, isn't it?'' Dr. Dan enclosed Mrs. Washington's hands in his own for a moment. Andy could see his magic working as Robbie's mother absorbed the confidence of his touch.

Mrs. Grymes stood up and moved to the door of the lounge. She pushed the door open, and a completely reassured Mrs. Washington followed her into the hallway.

Just as Andy was about to step in front of Dr. Dan and follow Robbie's mother out of the lounge, he stopped her by placing both his hands on her shoulders. He surprised her totally when he pulled her close and hugged her tightly to his crisp, white coat. Andy felt her knees go weak. Her heart paid no attention to her brain and began to race and thump madly. She fought the almost overpowering desire to throw her arms around his neck and hug him back.

"Andréa, Andréa, what you did today was wonderful. I know you're too modest to take the credit you deserve. I'm so proud of you. So proud. Robbie needed you, and you did everything right. You're going to be one of the finest nurses Bayshore Medical has ever produced.'' He hugged her again, then let her go.

"I . . . I . . . . Thank you, Dr. Dan. I hope so.''

"No, Andréa, thank you, And I know so.'' He moved into the hall where Mrs. Grymes stood waiting, her stiff face an unreadable stony mask. Had she seen Dr. Dan's hug?

"Mrs. Grymes?''

"Yes, Doctor.''

"You've got a fine nurse here, you know.''

"Yes, Doctor. I know. Andrea is one of my best. I can almost always count on her. Thank you.'' Even before Andy's supervisor had finished thanking him for his compliment to them both, he was moving down the corridor with his usual long strides.

Mrs. Washington, who was waiting to speak with him as he'd requested, had to hurry to keep up with his pace. She scurried along behind, until they both disappeared through the doorway to his conference room.

"I want to second what the doctor said, Andrea. You did a very competent job with Robbie and Mrs. Washington. Given time, I'm sure, you will make a highly qualified nurse. But until then, shouldn't you be taking Eric his afternoon bedpan?"

So much for pats on the back—and hugs. Back to bedpans—and the realities of being a nurse, thought Andy.

"Good use of your NIT-wits, Andrea," muttered Mrs. Grymes as she walked off briskly.

"Yes, ma'am. Thank you," gurgled Andy. If she says NIT-wits to me one more time—just one more time!—I'm going to give *her* Eric's bedpan, right in the . . . the . . . NIT-wits!

The warm water cascaded through the bedpan rinsing away the bubbles of antiseptic soap. Andy watched the bubbles swirl, forming a whirlpool, before flushing away to the Pacific Ocean. She'd never noticed how beautiful they could look before—all blue and red and yellow—so sparkly in the reflected light of the overhead fixture. Bubbles, she decided, made her happy, just as hugs made her happy. And hugs from Dr. Dan made her happiest of all.

"You're acting like a fool, Andrea Leigh Whitman," she berated herself. No. Not Andrea—Andréa. "Andréa Whitman. . . . Miss Andréa Leigh Whitman. . . . Mrs. Andréa Whitman Stewart. . . ." Well, Andy, old girl, it seems you're an even bigger dope than I thought. Just what are you planning to do with the present Mrs. Doctor Daniel Stewart? Or had you conveniently forgotten she exists? Andy shook her head and scrubbed the already clean pan even harder, speeding the last of the bubbles on their way in a sea of self-annoyance.

Daniel Stewart must care for her. He hugged her, didn't he? He must feel something. Did he sense how much she admired him? More than just admired him? Mrs. Evelyn Stewart wasn't even a nurse. How could she possibly understand a man, a doctor, with his deep dedication and great talent? And how could he really love a woman who didn't understand him? She'd never even seen Mrs. Stewart in pediatrics. Wouldn't a woman who had an interest in her husband's life come to see him at his work once in a while? She knew *she* would! If Andy were a doctor's wife, she knew she'd want to see him working, making his commendable contribution to the improvement of the human condition. She would watch and admire him from the sidelines, as he saved the lives of children who loved him. That's what she'd want to do.

"And guess what, dope? That's exactly what you're going to do: Watch him! Nothing else! And if you don't forget this silly crush you have on Daniel Stewart, it's going to break your heart. Find someone else, Andy, someone who can care for you, too, someone you can love who can love you back." She listened to her own words, and she knew she was giving herself sound advice. But who would she find? Who could compare with Daniel Stewart? Who could she possibly find to love—and to admire? Most of the guys she met were of Joe Duffy's caliber, one small step up—from a bedpan!

The Little Small Jealousy

"OH, NO. NOT again! Not after the day I've had," moaned Andy. "It's not fair."

"Not again what? What's not fair?" asked Jackee. She scanned the hospital parking lot for some clue to Andy's dismay.

"Him. Over there. There's just so much Joe Duffy I can cope with," sighed Andy.

"Oh, yeah? How much is he offering, and can I have your leftovers?"

Jackee's confused look made it clear she was still uninformed about the latest Whitman-Meets-Duffy-on-the-Bus confrontation. Andy decided to leave it like that. "Believe me, Jack. You don't want him. Pretend you don't see him. Maybe he'll just leave."

"I really don't think that's going to happen, Andy. In case you haven't noticed, that adorable yellow Volkswagen that his attractive, tall, sexy frame's draped all over happens to be the very vehicle we are planning to depart in."

What Andy did notice, to her consternation, was that Jackee didn't seem the least bit disconcerted. She on the other hand, wished to scream. And she didn't think it was just her imagination—but the slower she tried to walk, the faster Jackee's pace increased. She needed a miracle. A little divine intervention would do. She prayed for something to happen, something small but cataclysmic. Nothing did. Maybe he's just a nightmarish apparition—from my disturbed psyche? Maybe he really isn't there at all? Maybe Jackee's psyche is as disturbed as mine and we're seeing the same delusion? And, pretty please, maybe he isn't waiting for me? She was running out of maybes almost as quickly as she was running out of parking lot separating her from the grinning, dreaded Joe Duffy.

"Hi there, beautiful and beautifulest." The "beautifulest" was said directly to Andy. "Nice car, Andy. Yours?"

"You know it's not. *I* ride the bus. Or don't you remember?" snapped Andy.

"Do I remember? How could I forget? Haven't I even tried several times to say I'm sorry about all that business on the bus? But you won't let me. I've even offered to play Peter Pan with you and protect you from nasty pirates. What more can I do?"

"Peter Pan?" asked Jackee. She looked from Andy to Joe.

"Never mind, Jack," Andy blurted, cutting off more questions. "I don't want to play anything with you, Joe Duffy. Not Peter Pan, and not humiliation time on the bus." But remembering how he'd behaved when she was reading to Robbie and Heather almost weakened her resolve. Almost, but not quite. She was still going to do her utmost to avoid him—no matter what.

"You're right. I knew this was your friend's car. I overheard you telling Mrs. Grymes you were getting a ride with Jacklyn Paige from geriatrics. Marvin, at the gate, told me which car was Jacklyn's." Joe's eyes seemed to search Andy's face as he talked.

"Well, there it is. You've seen her car. I've confirmed Marvin's identification, and he told you the truth. You can go."

The glare of his blue eyes was so intense that Andy felt she'd be burned by his stare. She looked away quickly.

"Your friend's lucky; this is a beautiful little machine." His obvious flattery didn't fool Andy for one minute. It fired her spirit and gave her the strength to return his searing look.

"You really like her?" Jackee's interruption didn't end the battle his blue eyes were waging with Andy's icicle green ones. "Ms. Buggy is my own golden chariot. Want to take a look inside?"

Jackee unlocked the door on the driver's side and leaned across the seats to open the passenger door for him.

"Oh, sure. Thanks," said Joe. His eyes never blinked.

"Help yourself. Andy can keep you company while you look her—I mean it—over. I have to go . . . go find Monica . . . Monica Ross, my roommate. She's always late. Take your time. Make yourself at home, Mr. . . ."

"Joe Duffy. Just call me Joe, Jacklyn. All my friends do. Right, Andy?" He grinned devilishly.

"Okay, Joe. If you call me Jackee, or Jack, or whatever you want. I'll answer to anything. Won't I, Andy?" Jackee took one look at Andy; the smile she'd given Joe fell off her face.

Andy just glared at them both. Jackee babbled on and on. Could she actually like Joe? She was obviously shoving them together. Andy intended to kill Jack—the first chance she got. "Joe's probably in a hurry to get home. I'm sure he doesn't want to see your car right now." She extended her hand to him, feeling foolish, like a queen ending an audience with one of her subjects. "Well, good night, then."

"Oh, I'd love to give this cutie the once-over." He smiled knowingly at Andy's discomfort. "I'll just keep Andy company, as you suggested, Jackee. Please don't rush on my account. I'm in no hurry at all," Joe assured her.

Andy felt her hands tighten into clenched fists. She counted to three. Jackee couldn't be that dense. She had to see how much she didn't want to be left alone with him. As Andy watched her friend practically skipping back toward the hospital entrance, she began counting to ten again—starting over from one.

"Look, Andy, I know you're still upset about that bus thing the other morning. Won't you please forgive me? Wendy always forgave Peter when he was naughty. Honestly, I didn't mean to embarrass you like that. I meant it as a joke. I guess I wasn't very funny, was I?" Andy would never have believed that Joe Duffy could look so sincere or sound so humble.

"No, I guess you weren't very funny to me. If I do as you ask. . . ? If I forget about what happened. . . ?"

"And forgive?"

". . . And forgive, will you stop bothering me?" To avoid the effect his eyes were having on her, Andy stared at his white tennis shoes. She wondered if Mrs. Grymes would call them sensible? "And no more jokes? Please."

"No more jokes. I promise. But, I'd still very much like to be your fiancé."

"Joe Duffy! You promised!" She said his name loud enough to cause passersby to turn and look. She closed her eyes for a minute, searching for that much-needed extra ounce of Nurse Whitman patience.

"Just Joe. And I wasn't joking, Andy. Not this time."

Her eyes shot open. His voice seemed a bit too serious. "I want to thank you for your offer, but I don't think so. Not tonight." She wanted this conversation about fiancés to stay light and to end light.

"No engagement tonight?"

"No engagement."

"Dinner and a movie tonight?"

"No dinner and a movie."

"Just dinner, then?"

"No dinner. I can't. Jackee, Monica, and I are going to have dinner together. This is the first time in a month we've had a night off together—without homework, exams, or aide duty. I couldn't back out on them now."

"Sure you could," announced Jackee. Andy was amazed to realize she'd been talking so pleasantly with Joe that she'd forgotten to listen for Jackee and Monica to come back and save her from him. Their sudden appearance startled her. "Sorry. Didn't mean to scare you. But honestly, Andy, if you want to go with Joe, Monica and I can party without you."

"Jackee's right. We really don't mind," added Monica, studying Joe, her head tilted to one side. Whatever she was considering so seriously, she must have made up her mind, because she finally gave Joe a big, friendly smile.

"I know you don't mind. But we've been planning tonight for weeks; I want to go with you. You understand, Joe?" She did truly

45

want to spend the evening with her friends. Although they seemed extremely anxious to push her off on him. Maybe they didn't want to have dinner with her. But that was silly. Of course they did, as much as she wanted to be with them. Still, there was this tiny, gnawing feeling in the farthest corner of her mind that said a dinner with Joe Duffy wouldn't really be so bad, would it? Yes, it would. It had to be. What was the matter with her, anyway? No Joe Duffy. She'd made that promise to herself—several times. Besides, he probably had the most deplorable table manners. She had planned a night out with Monica and Jackee, and she was going to have a night out with Monica and Jackee—period! So why did she feel so regretful?

"Sure, ladies. I understand. Well, I've kept you long enough. I'd better be going, too. It was nice to meet you, Jackee, Monica."

"I'm afraid we weren't really formally introduced. I'm Monica Ross. And it's nice to meet you too, Joe Duffy."

"Joe. Just Joe. Me too, Monica. Be seeing you, Handy Andy." He gave them a smile that crinkled up the corners of his eyes and showed two rows of even, sparkling white teeth. Both Jackee and Monica returned his smile and waved, a bit too enthusiastically to suit Andy.

Andy wanted to wave. Her hand, poised in midair, hung there.

"Wow, Andy. Where did you get him? He's darling, isn't he, Jack?" Monica pressed the back of her hand to her forehead and faked a proper Victorian swoon. "He is just too, too dee-vine," came her attempt at a high-toned British accent. She hopped into the back seat of the VW and collapsed into an equally proper Victorian faint.

"Too, too," agreed Jackee. She and Monica rocked the small car with their giggles.

"First of all, you two, I didn't get him anywhere." Andy slipped into the front seat, pulled the door closed, and strapped on her safety belt. "In fact, I don't even have him." She settled back in her seat with a sigh.

"Then what was all that talk about a bus, and wanting to apologize to you? And what about Peter Pan?"

"Peter Pan," echoed Monica.

Andy hesitated before answering Jackee's question.

"And I heard that sigh. Come on, Handy Andy. Spill all," coaxed Jackee. Her gold-flecked eyes narrowed with curiosity.

"Yes, tell us, Andy. We think he's great. He's real sweet, and cute, too. I love his curls; makes him look like . . ." Monica seemed to be searching for just the right words.

"Peter Pan," Andy whispered under her breath.

"What? Never mind. He's adorable, that's all. What's going on between you two?" Monica leaned forward as if expecting to hear some earth-shaking revelations.

"Yeah, what?" Jackee mirrored Monica's avid interest.

"Oh, all right. If you really want to know . . . ?"

"We really do," panted Jackee. "Handy Andy and Peter Pan?"

"To be honest, I really didn't like Joe Duffy, the *needling* phlebotomist. . . ."

"Didn't like Joe?" Monica asked surprised.

"I didn't like Joe! Okay? He's kind of a pain. Always hanging around, teasing me, and making jokes. Like calling me Handy Andy, which he knows I hate, even on pedi-3. A couple of times he's really ruffled Simon LeGrymes's feathers, and I've landed in trouble—simply because I was standing next to him! Then, a few days ago, you guys had afternoon duty and were driving in too late, so I rode the early bus—remember? The day I got the croissants from Mr. Pakkala?"

"I remember you rode the bus. I never saw the croissants. I never got one," Monica informed Andy disappointedly.

"You don't need one. You're on a diet, remember? Forget the croissants. What about the bus?" Jackee urged impatiently.

"Well, I was so busy talking to Mr. Pakkala, I almost missed the bus. And then . . ." ̄

"That's fantastic. I love it," announced Jackee when Andy had finished her story.

"Joe Duffy sounds sensational," Monica bubbled. "Boy, are you ever dumb having dinner with us when you could be with him."

"I'm where I want to be," confirmed Andy.

"We all are," shouted Jackee, whipping the tiny car into an even

47

tinier parking space at the curb, with a flick of her wrist. "Little Small Café, here we come. Out of my way. Suddenly I'm starved."

"You drive like an entrant in the Indy 500. One of these days you're going to run this yellow bomb into something a lot bigger than Ms. Buggy, and—*kaboom!*" teased Monica. "You should be required to provide air-sickness bags back here."

"Everything is bigger than Ms. Buggy. And I haven't hit anything yet."

"Dumb luck," suggested Andy. Laughing, the three girls entered the dimly lit Belgian restaurant.

"Wait here. I'll tell Monsieur León we have arrived," said Monica.

Andy and Jackee took seats in the small foyer.

Slowly Andy's eyes adjusted to the soft glow of flickering candlelight that was so much a part of the café's charming atmosphere. The café hummed with faceless voices. Then one of the lush green ferns resting on an antique plant stand shimmered into focus. Silhouetting it, a barely illuminated stained glass window glowed. The café was a delight to the eye as well as an epicurean treat. Romantic music, softly strummed by the café's guitarist, completed the mood. Best of all, there was Monsieur León, the rosy-cheeked and slightly rotund Belgian owner, who made sure lovely ladies never went unkissed. He never served a less than perfect meal, and the prices stayed in a range that even an N.I.T. could afford—sometimes. The Little Small Café was total perfection and, little wonder, the three friends' favorite place to have dinner on special occasions.

"Hi, Monsieur León," Jackee greeted the owner, who had returned with Monica.

He kissed Jackee on both cheeks and whispered, "*Ma chère* Mademoiselle Jacqueline." Next it was Andy's turn. "Mademoiselle Andréa." Monsieur León placed a kiss on each of her cheeks, also.

Andréa! Why did her name sound so special when someone pronounced it like that? Why wasn't there someone special who looked at her, Andy Whitman, and saw Andréa? Why couldn't there be someone like Dr. Dan in her life to bring her to the Little Small Café and share its romance with her? *"Merci, Monsieur,"* she said, kissing the little man on his round pink cheeks in greeting.

"Ah, bien. Bien. Avec moi, s'il vous plaît." He led them to one of his best tables and presented their menus with a courtly bow. *"Bon appétit, mes petites chou-choux,"* he said, slipping away to give them time to make their selections.

"What's a *piteet shoe-shoe?*" asked Monica. "Is that good?"

"He called us his little cabbages," explained Jackee, who, in spite of her ongoing game of using atrocious French with Monsieur León, spoke the language beautifully. "It's a very special endearment in French. It's very good. Now decide what you want so we can order. I'm getting faint."

The next twenty minutes were taken up with several *I'm not sures* and *what are you going to haves?* At last the order was given to the waiter.

Andy's saumon en croûte, the Wellington crust flaky and the mushroom paté thinly layered over a pink salmon fillet, was elegant and delicious. She shared bites with Jackee, who offered her veal to sample. They practically had to beg Monica to let them taste her bouillabaisse, the specialty, but she finally took pity on their long faces and relented. She accepted the tastes they offered, without qualms.

The choice for dessert was astonishingly easy to make: mousse tarte au chocolat. Each piece of Monsieur León's delicacy contained a zillion calories. It had to be shared three ways—one piece only. Each girl savored one tiny nibble at a time and carefully gauged the size of the nibbles taken by the other two. Finally came coffee belgique.

Andy couldn't help running her tongue over her spoon to be sure she'd gotten every drop of mousse tarte. She'd figured out—by averaging the number of bites she'd had from the last four slices of tarte they'd ordered on their last four very special occasions—that they were each entitled to six nibbles apiece. When she'd finished her second small bite, or even her first, that had seemed like a lot. But now that she was finishing her fifth one, she mourned the rapid disappearance of the dessert.

49

"I'm afraid it's your turn, Monica," she reminded, trying to sound gracious and knowing she'd fallen short.

Monica wasn't paying the slightest attention to Andy or the tempting confection before her. "Oh, that's okay, Andy. You eat it."

Monica said that? She must be coming down with something. "Here you are, Jackee," Andy offered, trying to be as fair as possible.

"Huh? Oh, no. You can have it." Jackee looked grim. Whatever Monica was coming down with, it looked as if Jackee was getting it too.

"What's going on? You're giving me *your* shares of tarte?"

"Nothing's going on. Absolutely nothing. Is it, Jack?" Monica didn't sound as if it was nothing.

"She's right, Andy. Absolutely nothing. I didn't see a thing," insisted Jackee.

Monica glared at her.

"See what? Where?" asked Andy. She swiveled in her chair to see what they were talking about. It didn't take her long to discover what was making her two friends so nervous.

"Andy, I—" stammered Jackee.

"You're right, Jack. There's nothing to see," Andy agreed, casually turning back to the table.

"You mean, you didn't see them?" sputtered Jackee. She plucked at one of the tiny curls at her neck, a habit when she was nervous.

Monica glared at her again.

"Oh . . . you mean *them?*" Andy hoped she sounded unconcerned.

"Yes, I mean *them.*" Jackee gave Monica a helpless smile.

"Then yes. I saw them."

"Who do you suppose that gorgeous redhead with Joe is?" whispered Monica. She glanced at Andy sheepishly, as if she wanted to take back her words.

"His mother?" quipped Andy, surprised at her own sarcastic tone.

"I really doubt that. And you can bet she's not his little brother, either," Jackee assured them.

"But it could be his sister," offered Monica hopefully. "Couldn't it?"

It was obvious, especially to Andy, that not even Monica believed that.

"You know, I think I've seen her before. Isn't she one of the big four? Those hot-shot nurses from surgery? I know one is a redhead. I hear she's fantastic in the operating room," said Jackee.

"Lucky Duffy," Andy uttered barely above a whisper. Her friends went on talking as if they hadn't heard. Andy was grateful to them. That had been meant as a nasty crack, and she had no reason to make it. She was acting like a spiteful and jealous girl friend, when she wasn't even sure if she and Joe were friends at all. She hadn't wanted to be, had she? That's what she'd said often enough. And thought. What was she saying now?

"Nothing that terrific looking is a nurse. I'll bet she's a fashion model. I would kill for her cheekbones," groaned Monica, puffing out her own cheeks to exaggerate their fullness. "And the rest of her too. That girl is positively willowy. She's tall, too."

"So what? I'm tall and willowy. Besides, I don't think she's that tall," announced Jackee indignantly. She tugged at a stray curl again.

"Jack, my dearly beloved roomie, you are tall and skinny. That is *not* the same thing," teased Monica.

"And if we eat any more dinners with Andy, I'm destined to stay that way forever."

"What did I do?"

"You consumed all the mousse single-handed. That's all," accused Jackee with mock anger.

"But . . . you both said you didn't want it!" exclaimed Andy.

"And you said you didn't want Mr. Joe Duffy, Esquire. Didn't you, Andy? But from the condition of that napkin you're twisting, I'd say you were having some second thoughts, too," observed Jackee.

Andy couldn't find the words to deny what Jackee said.

"Okay, that's enough seriousness. This is our night to have some fun. To kick up our heels. To howl. Andy, you forget about Joe Duffy. Jack, you forget about the tarte. I think Andy did us a big favor by eating it. Less for the lips means less on the hips. Let's pay our bill, grab our coats, and take Ms. Buggy to visit the Chocolate Ship Cookie. We can party with Liz and watch the harbor lights." Monica was trying her hardest to put their special occasion dinner back on a happier note.

Andy appreciated her efforts, but she was suddenly overcome with weariness. "I'm sorry. I guess I'm beginning to feel the effects of an exhausting day. Would you mind very much dropping me off at my house first? I'm afraid I'm just too tired to be good company." Andy smiled weakly. She wasn't sure whether Jackee and Monica believed her excuse for wanting to go home. It didn't matter. She knew it was true. All of a sudden she was tired—totally and completely worn out. All she wanted to do now was go home, so she could start forgetting about Joe Duffy and his gorgeous redhead.

6

Why? Why? Why?

ANDY STRAIGHTENED HER desk and stacked her books as she waited for her friend Gabriella Ortiz to finish talking to their biology professor. Gabby, who wanted to specialize in psychiatric nursing when she finished the nurse-in-training course, seemed to put in twice as much time on her studies as Andy and their other N.I.T. friends did. During her rotation in emergency, Gabby had discovered the Bayshore Clinic Crisis Center. She'd volunteered to work the crisis hot line for runaways one evening when the regular girl who spoke Spanish went into labor and had to leave her post unexpectedly. The Crisis Center and Gabby were perfect for each other. She'd found the area of nursing, she told Andy, where she knew she would get a chance to do something really valuable. Something for people who had no one else and who needed her. She'd even volunteered to work part-time on the crisis hot line for experience when she wasn't on N.I.T. duty at the clinic. There was no doubt in Andy's mind that her friend Gabby had chosen a hard road to follow. She carried more than her share of major responsibilities: at home with her large, fatherless family; at school, with an exceptionally heavy schedule of classes; and with her nurse-in-training work in the clinic. Still she found the time for all the countless people in physical and mental anguish who called out for help by phoning the Crisis Center's overworked hot line. Andy was convinced that Gabby would be wonder-

53

ful in her chosen medical field. She had what it took to be a nurse inside, where it counted.

There never seemed to be enough time in an N.I.T.'s busy schedule for indulging in casual conversation, and Andy looked forward to her walks from biology class to the hospital with Gabby, as a special treat. But what Andy had to discuss with Gabby today couldn't be called casual.

"You must be very sure, Andy. That's a serious accusation to make. If you're wrong, you'll be letting yourself in for a heap of troubles," warned Gabby. There was no mistaking her real concern.

"How can I be sure?"

"Has the little girl actually told you her mother hurts her?"

"Well, not in so many words," admitted Andy.

"Abused children rarely do. In most cases, the kids love the parent, and in spite of the pain inflicted on them, the kids want to protect them. And sometimes they're just too afraid to tell anyone what's happening to them," explained Gabby sadly.

"I don't know what to think. She was so frightened, almost terrified, when I told her that her mother would come to see her after her tonsillectomy. And Gabby, what about all those bruises on her arms? Her name is Heather, and she's as tiny as a little flower. She seems so frail. When she cried with such pathetic sobs, it broke my heart." Andy felt her eyes misting at the memory.

"But she could have been crying because of the surgery. Andy, you don't know for sure. You can't be certain she was crying because she didn't want her mother with her. You can't go around accusing every mother whose kid doesn't seem to like her of being an abusing parent. Is she bruised or badly scarred on other parts of her body, besides her arms? You've seen what kids can do to themselves just playing."

"I'm not sure. But if you could've seen her, Gabby. She was sobbing. I held her. I patted her thin little body and smoothed her tangled hair. I can't imagine a parent abusing such a sweet child. She's as pretty as a baby doll with her blonde hair and blue eyes. Why, Gabby? Why?"

"It doesn't matter how many abuse cases we get in Crisis, I'll

54

never understand why. Andy, it doesn't matter if the child is adorable or not, a good kid or a pain; some parents can't handle having children. They're sick, and they need help.''

"I don't know what to do."

"Isn't there anyone in pediatrics you could confide your suspicions to? The floor nurse, maybe? A few bruises might not make anyone take notice, but when you add Heather's behavior. . . . Then, if you both come to the same conclusions go to Dr. Dan or Mrs. Grymes. If there's a chance you're right, you'll have to report it," said Gabby.

"Maybe I should go to them first," said Andy. "Let them handle it.''

The two girls stopped in front of the sprawling two-story clinic where Gabby trained and worked. The words painted on the glass doors said Bayshore Medical Clinic, below that Life Crisis Counseling Center, then Hot Line, followed in big black letters, by Open 24 Hours.

"Handle what?" Gabby's dark eyes were serious. "I'd be very sure first. We're nurses. Nurses do not deal in assumptions; they deal in facts. Heather is perfectly safe while she stays in the hospital." Suddenly Gabby frowned pensively. "Haven't you ever wondered why Heather's staying longer than usual for a simple tonsillectomy?"

"I thought it had something to do with her blood clotting or slow healing. Now I don't know," said Andy, shaking her head.

"Well, as long as she's under a doctor's care she'll be safe. If I were you, I'd talk to Heather—a lot. And watch her when her mother is there. You can tell plenty by observation. Before you point any fingers, remember that one frightened outburst doesn't necessarily mean an abused child. There must be someone who can help you keep an eye on Heather. Someone she likes and trusts enough to talk to about this," suggested Gabby.

"Yes. I think I know someone she's really very fond of. He's the phlebotomist on my floor. All the kids seem to be crazy about him. I'll get his opinion before I do anything," promised Andy. The thought occurred to her that the bruises should have been noticed by

Joe when he took Heather's blood samples. Had he seen them but dismissed them? She would have to talk with him as soon as possible.

"Please let me know what you come up with. If what you suspect is true, we can help Heather's mother in the clinic. Bayshore Medical Center and I run a numero uno Crisis Center. We can fix anything." Gabby smiled, and the sparkle of hope in her dark brown eyes gave Andy a feeling of renewed confidence and determination.

"I will," promised Andy.

"*Hasta luego,* Andy. *Buena suerte.*"

"Huh? Oh, thanks. I could use a little luck, *mi amiga.*" No one ever graduated from the Santa Monica school system without learning a little Spanish. And that's how much Andy had actually mastered—a little. "I don't even want to think about the trouble I could be letting myself in for." Andy grimaced as a picture of Joe's grinning face flashed through her mind. Was she actually going to ask him for his help? She had to. Heather was far more important than any silly squabbles they might be having.

"It's going to be fine, so don't worry. I may be wrong, but I think you're going to find you're not alone in your suspicions," soothed Gabby.

"I'll do whatever I have to to help Heather. But after I talk to Joe, I may be the one who needs help."

"What?" Gabby looked puzzled. "Is that a riddle? Never mind. You can tell me later; I'm going to be late for work. *Adios,* Andy."

"*Adios,* Gabby. *Y muchas gracias.*" Andy was speedily exhausting her limited Spanish vocabulary. She waited until the short girl with glossy, waist-length black hair and the cherubic face disappeared through the clinic's glass doors. After a fast peek at her small digital wristwatch, Andy began to run. She had six minutes and eleven seconds to make it to pediatrics on time.

The first thought that came to Andy's mind as the stainless steel elevator doors slid open was that Mrs. Grymes had to be waiting for her. It couldn't be a coincidence that *her* N.I.T. supervisor was waiting in front of *her* elevator and staring at the huge-faced wall clock over the floor desk at the very moment *she* stepped out—with only three minutes left until she was late for duty.

Mrs. Grymes backed up to allow the passengers for the third floor to exit the car. When the elevator began its climb to the fourth floor, Mrs. Grymes wasn't on it.

"Could I be mistaken, Andrea? Don't you have duty at two?"

"Yes, ma'am. So I really have to hurry. I've only got"—Andy looked intently at the round clock on the wall behind her supervisor—"two more minutes."

"Well, when you have a little more time, Andrea, I think we should talk." There was no hint to her mood in the expression on Mrs. Grymes's face. Drat! And double drat! A punctuality lecture, I'll bet, thought Andy.

"Yes, Mrs. Grymes. I'll see to it." Yes, Mrs. Grymes. No, Mrs. Grymes. You must be slipping, Mrs. Grymes. You forgot to mention my NIT-wits, Mrs. Grymes. Andy hurried off toward the nurses' lounge.

"NIT-wits, Andrea. NIT-wits." Mrs. Grymes's last-minute reminder followed her through the door, echoing loudly behind her.

Eeek! Score one more for the supervisor, Andy shrieked inside her head. She was so angry she forgot the combination to her locker. After several tries she heard the releasing click and yanked open the tall metal door, sending it crashing into the locker next to hers.

"Grymes?" asked Dina Johnson, one of the regular pediatric nurses. Andy hadn't noticed her resting on the small green couch when she'd rushed into the lounge.

"Grymes," agreed Andy with a smile, feeling a little foolish that her childish tantrum had been observed. But the older nurse began to laugh, and Andy couldn't help joining her. Dina had been an N.I.T. too, once. She knew all about supervisors.

Her trim white cap in place, Andy smiled a good-bye to Dina and hurried to the floor desk to get her rounds assignment. She quickly glanced over the folder and headed for room four, her first stop. She'd taken only a few steps when she was struck by the awesome silence of the usually bustling and noisy pedi-3. The chirruping and chattering of children's voices seemed to have been stilled. Only the hum of regular hospital routine could be heard filtering down the empty halls. It gave Andy an eerie feeling of foreboding.

A woman's voice blared forth from room four, shattering the floor's unnatural stillness. Andy was startled and alarmed; the voice was loud and angry, edged with desperation. The screaming was garbled—words yelled on top of words, making no sense. Andy was running even before she heard the final, gasping shout.

"Heather!"

Not Heather! Not Heather! Please, not Heather, she prayed.

Andy immediately recognized the woman at Heather's bedside as Mrs. Berk, the child's mother. She was so shocked by what the woman was doing to the limp and terrified little girl that she stopped, stunned and disgusted.

Mrs. Berk clutched Heather by the shoulders and shook her so violently that Andy gasped in outrage. "Stop that this instant," shouted Heather's mother. "Stop that now!"

Tears streamed down the child's cheeks, but no sound could come from her small mouth so soon after her tonsillectomy. The choking, gurgling noises Mrs. Berk shook from her tiny daughter were horrifying.

Andy raced to the child's side. But before she could reach the hysterical woman and put an end to Heather's torture, she saw specks of blood appear on the little girl's trembling lips. Andy feared she'd begun to hemorrhage. Instinctively, she punched the medical emergency button over Heather's bed for help.

She literally sprung at Mrs. Berk, anxious to pull her away from the bed—and from Heather. She grasped and tugged. She tried yelling. She tried speaking to the woman with calm, reassuring words. Nothing could convince the completely out-of-control Mrs. Berk to release her grip on Heather's shoulders. Andy was locked in a desperate struggle of wills as she labored to pry the mother's fingers from their deadly hold. As Andy prevailed, the woman's fingers began to slip; slowly she let go, collapsing in a heap at Andy's feet. Ignoring the incoherent, sobbing creature on the floor, she gently lifted the terrified child into her arms and held her close. She stroked her, crooning quiet, comforting, soft sounds to the petrified little girl.

Only minutes passed before John Fricker, the doctor on duty, ran into the room, followed by several of the nurses. Within seconds Dr. Dan, Dr. Lacey Keiku from ob-gyn, whom he often consulted with, and Mrs. Grymes also answered Andy's emergency call. She relinquished Heather to their capable hands.

Andy took a deep breath and tried to think rationally. With rationality came realization—Robbie! She'd forgotten all about him. She rushed to his bed to find him huddled under his blankets, crying his heart out. Over and over he sobbed Heather's name. Andy eased back his covers and held out her arms to him. He looked up at her, his luminous black eyes filled with terror and tears. She took the weeping little boy from his bed and cradled him in her arms.

She felt it would be best to take Robbie out of the room, but to do that she would have to pass Heather's now subdued, but still crying mother. Holding his small body tightly to her own, his damp face burrowing into her protective shoulder, she walked to the door. Her one objective was to take Robbie away, as quickly as possible, from the terrible scene he'd just witnessed.

Stepping around Mrs. Berk's crumpled form, Andy heard the words the woman repeated again and again. Through muffled tears, she tried to explain the unexplainable: her totally inconceivable actions. Surprisingly, her words seemed filled with real pain and anguish: "I never meant to hurt her. I love my little girl. I never meant it. I love her. I love her."

The catch that rose up in Andy's throat threatened to choke her, and the tears that welled up behind her eyes came very close to breaking through her defenses and spilling free. Gabby had been right, after all. But that didn't make it fair. If there were parents who just couldn't handle the responsibility of having children, then Mrs. Berk was one of them. Anger raged in Andy. Mrs. Berk was sick, and Andy was a nurse; she should be able to understand illness. But not child abuse. Never! Searching her heart for some semblance of compassion for the distraught woman on the floor, she found only enough for the child, and nothing for the mother—a strange word to describe someone like Mrs. Berk.

"Why did Heather's mama get so mad at her, Andy?" asked Robbie between tearful hiccups. They sat together in the old over-sized chair in the nurses' lounge, his arms still snuggly clasped around her neck.

"I don't know, Robbie, honey. I only wish I did."

"I'm afraid of Heather's mama. She hurt her and made her cry. Heather doesn't like her mama, and neither do I. Make her go away, Andy. Okay? You tell her to go home," he sniffled.

"You don't have to be afraid anymore. Dr. Dan and Dr. Fricker are with your little friend. They'll take care of Heather, and they won't let anyone hurt her again. Here. . . ." She took a tissue from her pocket and helped Robbie wipe his eyes and blow his nose. "All better?"

Huge black eyes, glistening with tears, opened wide under Andy's gaze. With unwavering trust in her promise that Heather was truly safe, Robbie nodded his head. "Better," he answered.

"Andrea." Mrs. Grymes's stern voice gave her a start. Andy and her tiny charge jumped in their seat.

"Yes, ma'am," she replied, getting to her feet, but still embracing Robbie in a big, warm bear hug. "Is Heather—?"

"Yes, dear. Why don't you take Robbie back to his bed and tuck him in with a nice story? . . . Heather's gone for a little visit with Dr. Dan, Robbie. You can wait for her, and while you do, Nurse Andy will read to you. Maybe even *Curious George*. Would you like that?"

"Uh-huh." Robbie looked at Mrs. Grymes with what Andy would have described as cautious appraisal. It wasn't often he'd seen the formidable N.I.T. supervisor so soft-spoken and smiling. For that matter, neither had Andy.

"After you feel things are . . . settled down, dear, would you please come to Dr. Stewart's office?"

That was two *dears* in a row. Two *dears* from Mrs. Grymes? She nodded in agreement. Amazed, she carried Robbie out the door her supervisor held open for them. Two *dears* in a row!

"First of all, Andréa, let me say that you never cease to amaze us with your mature, quick thinking and your competent reactions to extremely difficult situations. You show the ability of a nurse with far more experience than you actually have. Although by now I should be accustomed to your frequent displays of nursing acumen." Dr. Dan's compliments were making her blush unmercifully. But if the doctor noticed her rosy coloring and her inability to reply, he chose to ignore it. "Don't you agree, Mrs. Grymes?"

"Yes, I do, Doctor. Like you, I am aware that Andrea is one of my best girls. Her work, for the most part, is exemplary. I'm quite pleased with her performance—so far." Mrs. Grymes delivered each sentence without the hint of a smile. Andy wondered if she hadn't imagined the earlier melting of her icy exterior. The two *dear*s had been replaced with a *one of,* a *for the most part,* and a *so far.* Still, from Mrs. Grymes that could be considered high praise indeed.

"I—I really don't know what to say," stammered Andy. Especially to Dr. Dan. "Thank you both, very much. I'll try to continue to make you proud of me."

"I have no doubt you'll succeed admirably." As the doctor smiled at her, Andy had the feeling that the smallest twitch of his upturned lip could melt an iceberg—even Mrs. Esther Grymes. "Now, Andréa, I would like to talk to you about Heather, and what happened here today with Mrs. Berk."

Andy bit her lip and nodded. She'd been planning to come to him with her suspicions about Mrs. Berk. But now that the matter was out in the open, she didn't know if she could bring herself to discuss it. It was so much uglier than she'd ever imagined it could be. She wished for the miracle that would give Dr. Dan all the answers to Heather's and her mother's problems. Then he could solve them, and everything would be all right. Yet in real life she knew that happily-ever-after was not that easy to find.

"When Dr. Fricker examined Heather, on admittance, he became quite concerned over several small bruises on the child. Mrs. Berk explained them away as the results of the usual, unimportant childhood mishaps. She mentioned that Heather had always bruised easily. But he was not entirely convinced, and he checked with Heather's regular pediatrician to see if he had ever noted any similar findings. Dr. Kendall, Heather's pediatrician, said that she'd never noticed anything that could be considered reasonable suspicion for an abuse charge against Mrs. Berk. Dr. Fricker checked every available source for any hint of possible child abuse, and he found nothing,'' explained Dr. Dan.

"After her surgery, there was a minor problem with Heather's healing, and that lent credence to Mrs. Berk's claim that her daughter bruised without much provocation.

"Dr. Fricker, Dr. Kendall, and I conferred with several other doctors, but I'm afraid that we could not reach a consensus. Although some of us felt there might be reason to suspect abuse, several of our colleagues disagreed completely.''

"You suspected the truth, didn't you? You should have done something,'' accused Andy angrily. She felt her faith in Daniel Stewart give way a little. She'd almost forgotten that he was human and that human beings make mistakes.

"We had nothing concrete to base our assumptions on, Andréa. It was a feeling. Only a hunch. Would you accuse an innocent person falsely because of a hunch?'' asked the doctor.

Wasn't that what Gabby had told her? Could she blame him for waiting? For wanting to be absolutely sure? She saw the genuine sadness that clouded his eyes, and the lines of worry that etched his brow. She knew he blamed himself.

"We've called the authorities. There'll be a very thorough investigation. But I promise you, Andréa, until this matter is resolved to my satisfaction, Heather will not be released from this hospital to her mother. Dr. Kendall, Dr. Fricker, and I have agreed to restrict her visitors; none will be permitted in her room without an attending nurse. No further physical or psychological harm will come to Heather while she's in this hospital.''

Andy felt relief replace her despair. The one thing she had fought so hard to resist, she could no longer control. With great, gulping sobs, she began to cry tears of release and understanding. She barely noticed Dr. Dan putting his arm around her to soothe her, until she'd cried herself out.

"One good thing did come from today," announced the doctor. He looked deeply into her tear-swollen eyes. His optimistic smile gave her strength. "Because of what happened today, we will have a chance to help Heather and her mother. It's a chance we almost missed."

Andy had to agree. That was definitely *one* good thing. Now that the tragedy in room four was over, Andy realized that *two* more good things had happened, also: Mrs. Grymes had forgotten all about their unfortunate meeting in front of the elevators and the impending lecture on punctuality; and there was no longer any reason for her to talk with Joe Duffy. That alone should have made her happy—but it didn't.

7

Broken Hearts and Handy Interns

SEEING ALBERT'S TINY mouth quivering, threatening to overcome his brave little smile, wrenched at Andy's heart. Of course he wanted to go home to his family. Of course she was glad he was well enough to leave the hospital. Still, she understood his mixed feelings about leaving pediatrics. She felt the same way each time one of her brood left her nest and went home. They were like a big family on pedi-3. Andy knew she would never forget a single one of her little chicks. There would always be a place in her heart for every child she'd cared for while she was an N.I.T. at Bayshore Medical Center. But on busy third-floor pediatrics there was never enough free time to enjoy the luxury of missing a patient; someone else would always fill the empty bed, and Andy had to allot a space for the newcomer in her hectic nursing schedule, and in her heart.

She waved and blew big kisses to the tearful but smiling boy in the wheelchair as she watched the heavy elevator doors slide closed. "Good-bye, Albert. Be good. Take care," she called, already missing him. She stood there watching until the floor indicator above the elevator doors blinked 2, then L. Albert's asthma was under control, and he was on his way home.

"You haven't seen Dr. Dan, have you, Andy?" asked the head nurse, Mrs. Wernick. "Admissions is already sending us Albert's replacement—an ulcer patient; his name is Sammy Inger. Let me tell you, there's never a dull moment or a minute's rest on this floor. I should have gone into professional football, as my father wanted me to."

"Professional football?" laughed Andy. "Not you?"

"There were times during my nurses' training when I actually considered it." Barbara Wernick's laughter mingled with Andy's, and a picture of Mrs. Grymes's face flashed before Andy's eyes. She knew exactly what Mrs. Wernick was talking about. "I guess I'd better page Dr. Dan before Sammy gets up here," mused the head nurse, thinking out loud.

"Oh, you don't have to, Mrs. Wernick. I saw him go into the lounge carrying his coffee cup, only a second ago. I'm going right by there. If you'd like, I'll get him for you."

"Would you, dear? Thank you." When she smiled, the head nurse for pedi-3 looked a little less harried.

"I'd love to, really. I'm already on my way," said Andy. She hoped the head nurse hadn't heard the excitement in her voice. Then Mrs. Wernick winked at her, and Andy felt her cheeks grow warm. Could everyone read her thoughts so easily? Well, Liz said there were a lot of nurses in Dr. Dan's fan club. Maybe even head nurses, too. After her talk with Liz, she'd been making an honest effort to stop letting her heart run away with her good sense. But she had to admit she'd had only limited success with her endeavor, so far.

Pushing open the door just enough to poke in her head, Andy peeked into the lounge. If he'd come in there for coffee, he didn't seem to be here now. "Are you in here, Dr. Dan?" she called. She waited, but no one answered her. Then, as she was stepping back to shut the door, Andy thought she heard a faint noise. She listened again. Thinking that the doctor might have decided to lie down on one of the larger couches, hidden behind the bank of lockers, and dozed off, Andy pushed open the door and went in.

"I'm sorry to bother you, Dr. Dan. But, Mrs. Wernick asked if you wou—'' The rest of the sentence slipped down into the pit of her stomach with a sickening thud.

"No reason to apologize, Andréa. Evie was just about to abandon me, anyway. Weren't you, darling?"

Andy tried not to notice the possessive way the doctor's strong hands spanned his wife's small waist. And the look of total contentment on their faces. She didn't belong there, and she wanted to run.

She tried backing out of the room but her feet wouldn't cooperate with her brain. "I—I—''

"Now, Dan, you know perfectly well that I have to be at the mayor's office in less than an hour to cover his weekly press conference. As much as I'd like to snuggle up with you on this old couch all afternoon, I'm a reporter with a very demanding editor and a deadline to meet. I have a job to do—even if you don't.''

Daniel Stewart beamed with pride at his pretty wife. "Oh, I'll bet Andréa's found something worthwhile for me to do. Right?''

Andy stood speechless.

"Dan, you dolt. Can't you see we're embarrassing the poor child? Let me get back to work. You're a doctor; be serious. Old married people don't hide behind lockers so they can neck with each other,'' insisted Mrs. Stewart. She kissed her husband, and the doctor grabbed her so she couldn't escape him while he kissed her back. Andy couldn't mistake the feelings behind their kiss. She'd been so wrong; Daniel Stewart loved his wife.

Andy wanted to be anywhere on earth except where she was. She was so ashamed. Her hand was on the door. Only one push and a few steps, then no one would be able to guess the foolish child she'd been.

"Andréa, what was it you wanted to tell me?"

She took a big gulp of air before trying to speak. "Mrs—Mrs. Wernick wanted you to know that your new ulcer patient, Sammy Inger, was on his way up from admissions." Her words spilled out; she had to get away.

She was not quite fast enough to avoid hearing the last noisy kiss Dr. Dan exchanged with his wife. I've been so *dumb, dumb, dumb.* And Liz, you were so right!

Andy heard the lounge door swish shut behind her. She squared her shoulders and took a deep breath. Now the door was also closed on any daydreams she'd ever had about the very handsome, very talented, and very, very married Dr. Daniel Stewart. She hurried off to tell Mrs. Wernick that the doctor was on his way. She'd found him and delivered the message. No trouble at all!

Andy was grateful that the rest of her morning passed in such a hectic blur. She had very little time to dwell on the painful picture of Mrs. Stewart in her husband's arms. She'd hoped that one day Daniel Stewart might come to think of her as something other than what she really was: a hardworking, competent, very young N.I.T. He'd never done anything to make her believe there was any relationship between them—other than doctor and nurse. And a very young, childish nurse, at that. Young, childish, stupid, and *dumb!*

When break time arrived, she was only too glad to leave the floor and head for the hospital cafeteria. She planned to treat herself to the gooeyest, most fattening thing she could find. Eating in the cafeteria could be hazardous, but the worst it could do was poison her and put her out of her misery altogether. There was a nasty rumor circulating through the hospital: that the cure rate of the patients at Bayshore Medical was remarkably high; but only one out of five people (even though they were mostly doctors and nurses) who ate in the hospital cafeteria survived the experience. If she could find a big enough piece of chocolate cream pie, Andy intended to throw caution to the wind, gobble up every crumb, then sit back and wait for her inevitable demise. Besides, after her harrowing experience that morning she felt she'd already lived enough to last two lifetimes.

"Crowded, isn't it?" asked the tall, attractive blond boy in line in front of her. Andy guessed he was about twenty-two.

She looked around. She was the only one near him, so he had to be talking to her. Andy smiled and moved her tray again.

"Anyone seeing this place for the first time might make the mistake of thinking people come here because the food is edible."

Andy laughed at his profound observation about the Poison Pit.

"My name's Collin. Collin Ellis. I'm an intern in med-surg—at the moment. I'm five feet eleven, one hundred and forty-five pounds, and I have all my own teeth. I live alone. I drive a Porsche Turbo, so you can see I'm not one of your usual starving-intern types. Although if I have to eat much more of this glop, I may be forced to become one. I can produce some very complimentary references as to my moderately substantial finances and impeccable ancestry. I'm desperately trying to impress you with my quick wit and clever repartee. So will you sit with me while you eat the horrible brown thing you have on your tray? And if you promise not to hold me responsible for what it does to your stomach, I'd even like to pay for it. What's your name? And please say yes."

"Andy Whitman. Yes, thank you."

They both burst out laughing.

Collin Ellis was very handsome—a different type of handsome from Daniel Stewart, for which Andy was very grateful. Maybe he could be the someone she needed to replace the person Liz had suggested as a possible candidate, to make her forget all about the happily married head of pediatrics. They found an empty table and sat down across from each other.

Andy nibbled at her too-sweet pie and listened while Collin told her all about himself and his totally planned future. He was quick to point out that he wouldn't be an intern forever.

"The real money," he explained, "is in specialization. I'm headed for a brilliant career in neurosurgery."

Andy only half listened as he talked. Her first instinct was to write Collin Ellis off as an immature braggart, and forget him. But that's what she was always doing lately: measuring every man she met against Daniel Stewart. They all seemed so young and shallow compared with him, and of course they all fell short. Not this time. In spite of herself, Andy was going to give Collin a real chance. Without making comparisons. She was probably jumping to conclusions about him, anyway. He was just trying especially hard to impress her. Instead of cutting him down for it, she should be flattered he was making so much of an effort on her behalf. For some reason he really seemed to want her to like him.

"So, what do you say?"

"About what?" Andy asked. She'd been so lost in her own thoughts she'd missed the question.

"About tonight? Anywhere you want to go. Is it a date?"

Andy studied the blond hair and hazel eyes of the young man across from her. He was very attractive—extremely so. She'd be a fool to turn him down. Hadn't she already been a big enough fool for one day? Say yes, she prodded herself. Go on—say it.

It's just that there was something about him that didn't feel right. Something she couldn't quite put her finger on. Had Samantha Crane ever mentioned him? He was an intern on Sam's service, in med-surg; she'd have to have met him. But if Sam had said something terrible about him, Andy was positive she would have remembered. And he did have a beautiful smile. . . .

"I'd like that. Would you like to go to Skating et Cetera? A few of my friends mentioned they'd be there tonight." She gave him her answer before she had a chance to change her mind.

"Roller-skating? I guess so. Sure. Why not? As I said, anywhere you want. Skating et Cetera it is."

Ten minutes later when Andy stepped off the elevator on the third floor, her date with Collin was all planned. They were going to have a super time. A spectacular time. It would be a date she would never forget. So why did that little voice buzzing in her ear keep asking her so many silly questions?

Are you sure you aren't making a mistake, Andy Whitman? Are you sure you aren't running away? Who are you really running away from?

The John Starr
Shoot-Out

ANDY HEARD THE rumble and felt the roar of his car as it pulled into the driveway. She didn't need the honk of his horn to tell her Collin Ellis had arrived. A fast glance into the mirror to double-check her lipstick and give a final fluff to her bouncy, brown curls, and she was all set. The old oak-framed mirror told her the same tale it always did: her lips were their usual Delectable Delite pink, her cheeks appropriately flushed, her nose powdered, her hair only slightly out of control.

"Well, Mr. Ellis, there is nothing more I can do. Take it or leave it," warned the image-Andy from the mirror. She winked and the image-Andy winked back; she was sure he'd take it. She wasn't so bad. She picked up her lipstick and compact from the dresser and dropped them into her pocket. Then she hurried down the hall to the front door, just as Collin honked again.

"Where do you think you're going, young lady?" called her dad. He lowered his newspaper to glare at her over the top.

"Roller-skating with Collin Ellis, an intern at the hospital; I told you, Dad."

Collin's horn blared several more times.

"That's what you said, all right. I'm probably just an old-fashioned kind of guy, but I'd like to meet this Collin what's-his-name. Especially if he intends to take my favorite daughter out in a growling, souped-up bomb." The hazel eyes that peered over the newspaper from behind Ben Franklin half-glasses delivered to Andy a very no-nonsense squint.

"For your information, I just happen to be an old-fashioned kind of girl. I was on my way to get Collin what's-his-name and invite him into the house so he could meet my wonderfully sweet and protective Dad. So there."

"Then go get him—before the neighbors have him arrested for disturbing the peace." Big Andy grinned at his daughter. "We wouldn't want any trouble with the law, would we?"

"I love you, Lieutenant Whitman," whispered Andy, planting a big kiss on his cheek. "You wait right here, and I'll go get him." She went out on the porch and waved to Collin to come in.

Andy tried not to see the look on her dad's face as Collin made his first impression. He walked in the door with his thumbs hooked in the pockets of his designer jeans. His step in his high-heeled boots was almost a swagger. She knew exactly what was going through Big Andy's mind. The truth was that Collin looked perfect—almost too perfect. His blond hair was meticulously cut and had obviously been professionally styled. His clothes were the "in" western look. His boots shone as only expensive, new leather could. But it was his attitude, more than anything else—his so-this-is-where-you-live glance around the room—that created the jagged edge. As her dad reached out and shook Collin's hand, Andy could guess from the way his eyes narrowed that Collin's grip didn't impress Big Andy much, either. He wasn't the type her dad called "a man's man." Suddenly she was filled with doubt. Why had she accepted this date in the first place?

Whatever her dad's thoughts, he was doing a good job of not letting Collin see them. Or maybe Collin chose not to notice? Or maybe he just didn't care what her dad thought of him? He seemed totally at ease, pumping Big Andy's hand, his broad smile displaying perfect white teeth.

"That's a pretty snazzy auto you drive, Collin." Big Andy made a point of taking a second long look out the window at the fiery red Porsche gleaming in the driveway. "You take it easy when my daughter's in it; it looks lethal."

"Sure thing, Lieutenant. No sweat. She isn't dangerous if I keep her under a hundred miles an hour. Andy's safe with me, sir."

Her dad didn't look completely convinced. "Dad. . . ." She wanted to say something that would reassure him. Something that would reaffirm his faith in her common sense and let him know that she would insist on Collin's driving safely. "We'd better go," she said, instead.

"It was my pleasure to meet you, Lieutenant Whitman. I'll take good care of Andy. I promise I'll get her back to you safe and sound." Once more, Collin shook hands with Big Andy.

Even though Collin hadn't done or said one single thing to displease him, Andy knew her dad didn't like her date very much. And, for Big Andy, that was the exception rather than the rule. She kissed his cheek a last time, then followed Collin out to his sleek Porsche.

The ride to the skating rink was exhilarating, even though Collin kept his word and never drove beyond the speed limit. Andy had never been in such a beautiful and expensive car before, and it was an exciting experience. She sat snuggly in her seat belt, her hands folded primly in her lap, and hardly heard the taped music from his stereo cassette player as she studied his profile.

She was bemused by the way different people responded to the same person. Andy had sensed immediately that her dad wasn't very taken with Collin Ellis. Yet earlier that evening when she'd called Sam to ask her what she thought of Collin, she'd gotten a completely different response.

Sam hadn't come home yet from the night class she was taking at the university, so Toddson the butler had put Samantha's grandmother, Morgana Crane, on the phone. Andy explained why she was calling, and Mrs. Crane wondered if she might know the boy in question; she was quite friendly with most of her granddaughter's friends. Although Andy doubted that Mrs. Crane would know an intern whom Sam merely worked with, she'd told her his name. And,

Sam's unflappable grandmother, who had never been known to have a single hair out of place, became totally unglued. She went into raptures, extolling the extraordinary qualities of every member of the Ellis family. She finished by saying, "And Collin, my dear, is a delightful and very charming product of good breeding and the fine Ellis environment. I would definitely encourage any granddaughter of mine to date young Ellis. I can't imagine why Samantha hasn't mentioned working with him at that place—that hospital. Tell me, dear, what kind of a physician is Collin planning to become?" When she'd explained all the things that Collin had told her about his future plans, the thought of Dr. Ellis, neurosurgeon, incited Mrs. Crane to even higher praise of his character.

Andy suddenly wondered if the very traits that caused Sam's grandmother to find Collin so acceptable might not be the ones that had turned her dad off? Well, now she had an opportunity to make up her own mind, and she promised herself not to let anyone else's opinions prejudice her decision.

Andy was a little disappointed that none of her friends were in the parking lot to see her arrive in Collin's Porsche. She had the feeling she looked sensational when she stepped out of the sports car. She'd been pleased when he'd complimented her on her fluffy powder pink sweater and matching slacks. But when she'd glanced up at him as he helped her from the car, his eyes had told her just how good she really did look—even more than his words had. .

As they stood in the short ticket line, Andy felt the beat of the music. She was eager to get into skates and glide rhythmically around the floor. The music didn't seem to be moving Collin in the same way. He seemed agitated as he paid for their tickets, fumbling with the change in the cash register return dish and muttering to himself when a few of the coins fell on the floor.

It had never occurred to her to ask him if he could skate. Maybe he was nervous about coming to the rink. But after he'd promised to take her anywhere she wanted to go, he'd probably felt obligated to bring her.

"You don't mind our coming here, do you? If you'd rather go somewhere else, I'm sure they'll give us the money back."

"Look, Andy. You said you wanted to come here, so don't worry about it. Besides, I've always wondered what the children of America were doing for kicks these days."

Andy decided not to pursue the discussion. Collin's apprehensive smile bothered her and, she thought, probably accounted for his surly tone.

They moved to the next counter and told the woman their shoe sizes. She handed them two pair of skates; Andy's were a flashy red, and Collin's much larger ones a sparkling blue. They sat down on a bench in front of a row of pay lockers and slipped them on. Collin handed Andy a quarter and she locked up their street shoes and gave him back the key. After several attempts to lace his skates properly, turning down her offer to help, he finally stood up.

"I wonder if you have the right size skates," said Andy. "Maybe they're too big?" She was trying to be tactful as Collin wobbled and swayed toward her, trying to maintain his balance.

"No, they're fine. It's been awhile since I've skated, that's all."

"Didn't you ever come here . . . when you were younger?"

"Once or twice. Frankly I didn't like it much . . . or bowling, either. I hate putting on shoes other people have worn. I didn't like it enough to buy my own skates; that's for sure. I've never been too interested in any sports—except sports cars, and skiing. I have my own ski equipment; I bought it in Switzerland."

"I used to have my own roller skates when I was little. But they weren't anything like these. Even the rink is different. I started coming here when it was the Santa Monica Roller Rink and you skated on a wood floor. Now it's Skating et Cetera—flashing lights, rock music, and a poly-something-or-other speed track. Roller-skating has come of age, as my dad would say."

"If you say so," said Collin, with none of Andy's enthusiasm.

Andy wished she hadn't asked him to bring her; things weren't turning out as she'd hoped.

"Hey! Andy! Over here." Someone was shouting at her over the blare of the loud rock music.

"Oh, look. There's Gabby and Liz. Come on; I'll introduce you to my friends." Andy took his hand, and they rolled to the nearest opening in the rink wall. They watched the skaters circling in front of them in time to the beat of the music, as they waited for Gabby and Liz to come back around.

"Girl, why didn't you say you'd be here tonight?" Liz executed a perfect axel, spinning gracefully in a complete circle. Stepping through the opening in the low wall, she gave Andy a hug.

Out of breath, Gabby had to slam into the wall to stop.

"But here we are," said Andy, too gaily. "Collin, I'd like you to meet Gabriella Ortiz and Elizabeth Jones. They're both N.I.T.s at Bayshore, too. Gabby, Liz, this is Collin Ellis."

"Aren't you an intern in med-surg? With Samantha Crane?" asked Liz. "I've heard your name."

"Yes, I am. We did come here to skate, didn't we, Andy? Will you ladies please excuse us?" He took Andy's hand and pulled her onto the shiny cobalt blue track.

Andy couldn't believe her ears. Collin hadn't said one impolite word, and he'd still managed to display the rudest behavior she'd ever seen. He'd actually cut Liz off, cold. She looked back at her open-mouthed friends, then up at Collin. "Don't you like my friends?"

"Of course. I'm sure they're terrific. Do all you little nits stick together? You seem to know one another so well."

"No, not all the N.I.T.s. But five of my closest friends are nurses in training at Bayshore Med. Aren't you friends with the guys you work with?" Andy could hear the angry edge in her voice.

"Some. Okay? . . . Look, I'm sorry I said anything." He smiled apologetically. "So what do you think of my skating ability now? I just needed to get my sea legs."

Andy hoped his smile was sincere; Collin Ellis was getting harder and harder to figure out. His whole personality seemed to improve as his agility on skates increased. His sullen expression changed to a wide, flashing smile. He confused her. Maybe she'd only imagined it. Maybe his behavior toward her friends wasn't rude. Maybe it was only his insecurity at having to skate in front of them that had made him seem so curt with Liz. When he squeezed her hand playfully and then sped up to lap the couple in front of them, Andy relaxed a little. She had to race to keep pace with him.

"Hi, Andy. *Qué pasa?* How about a little tripping the light fantastic on the next disco skate?" asked the young Latino who skated past them backward.

Andy shrugged and smiled.

"Who was that?" asked Collin "Another nit?"

"That was Tonio, Gabby's brother. He's a great skater."

"What's he do, hang around here with all the little kids every night? He looks a little old for roller-skating."

"What's old, Collin?"

He didn't answer.

"He's only in his middle twenties. He brings Gabby and sometimes their little sister, Matia. Gabby's mother doesn't let her go out alone at night. She's kind of overprotective, because of the neighborhood they live in, and because Gabby's father is dead."

"You're kidding! And she's going to be a nurse? Look, let's get out of here, okay? I think I've had enou . . . FFF!" Before he could finish his sentence, Collin found himself on his backside, with Andy bending over him.

"Hey, man. Can I help?" offered Tonio. He seemed to appear out of thin air, making a fast toe stop beside Andy. He extended his hand to Collin.

"No, thanks. I can manage," Collin hissed, hoisting himself to his feet with a grunt. "Can we go now?" His eyes were angry yellow marbles as he took Andy's hand and dragged her off the track.

"Andy?" he said sheepishly. She knew he was testing the extent of her anger. "Andy?" he said a bit louder. "Hey, I'm really sorry about the way I acted back there. As I said, I'm not much for athletic endeavors. I guess all those little kids outskating me made me feel stupid." His look was so pathetic and his apology sounded so sincere that she had to accept it. He gunned the Porsche engine as they waited for the red light to flash green.

"That's okay. If you weren't having a good time, I wouldn't have wanted to stay either."

"Why don't we go get something to eat? Are you hungry?" The old Collin was back. "The night is still young, as they say."

"Who says?"

"She says. You know: 'She says sea shells down by the she shore.' "

"Collin, that's ridiculous. It's 'she sells sea shells down by the sea sore—shore!' I meant 'shore.' " They were finally laughing together, the strained atmosphere of the skating rink melting away.

"Well? Do we eat?"

"We eat. Where?"

"Right here." He pulled the car into the parking lot of a restaurant whose front gave the impression of an old western town. Narrow wooden stores with fake signs and painted windows were lined up side by side. But the door off the parking lot was real, and that's where Collin was leading her.

"I can't go in there, Collin. The John Starr Saloon—it's a real bar. I'm not old enough to go into a bar."

"You really do hang around with little kids, don't you? Don't worry; they also serve food. As long as you don't go to the bar and demand service, there won't be any trouble. I promise; no one's even going to notice you're here."

It didn't take Andy long to see that Collin had been telling her the truth. No one seemed to notice her. But they did notice Collin. He seemed to know just about everybody in the dimly lit and smoky John Starr, and they seemed to know him. At a table near the back of the room, away from the bar but right on top of the dance floor, Collin squeezed in two more chairs. The table was already filled to overflowing with people, but they didn't seem to mind and they welcomed him loudly. Andy noticed immediately that she was several years younger than anyone else at the table. She was introduced, but there were so many names and Collin went so fast that she could remember only a few. No one seemed to remember hers, not even the people who'd stopped talking and drinking long enough to hear his introduction. There weren't many who did.

"What'll ya drink, sweetie?" asked a pretty waitress in tight jeans and an even tighter cowboy shirt. She was wearing too much makeup, but with her black Stetson tipped over one eye and a red bandanna tied around her neck, the waitress looked very sexy, Andy thought. She looked down at her own kitten soft sweater and slacks—her favorite outfit. When she wore it, she always felt her best and thought she looked her best, too. But at the John Starr, she only looked out of place.

"I—ah—nothing right now, thank you," she stammered. She could have ordered a coke. And on special occasions she'd even have a glass of white wine. But this was definitely not an occasion —at least not one she'd want to remember. What was she doing here? she asked herself. Well, she certainly wasn't going to stay. "Collin. . . . Collin?"

He was having a deep conversation with the girl next to him, who was wearing a leather, Indian-style vest, and no shirt. He either couldn't, or wouldn't hear her over their talking and the loud music.

"Collin, please. I think we should go." She practically shouted to be heard.

"Sure, Andy. Right away. Here . . . drink this and relax for a couple of minutes. We just got here. At least let me finish talking to Dee." He pushed a tall glass toward her.

"All right. But only a minute. What is this? Soda?" The drink he'd passed to her looked like ordinary cola with ice cubes and two straws.

"Yup, just like soda pop. Finish it. You'll like it." He turned his back to her and resumed his conversation with the scantily dressed Dee. How did she have the nerve to leave her house dressed like that? wondered Andy.

Andy hesitated. She'd told him she didn't drink. He wouldn't have given it to her if it wasn't soda. She took a sip and wrinkled her nose. He not only thought she was a little kid, but a very stupid little kid, too. She pushed the glass back at him. "Collin, I'm going home."

"Not unless you want to walk. I'm not ready to leave." He barely even looked at her. His thin veneer of courtesy was rapidly wearing away.

"I didn't say *we;* I said *I* was leaving. You can stay. . . . For-

78

ever, if it makes you happy. I can call a cab." Andy pushed back her chair as far as it would go and struggled to stand up. She was almost up when Collin grabbed her arm to stop her from leaving.

"Give me a chance to say good-bye. I said I'd take you home," he snarled at her.

"No, thank you. I'd rather call myself a cab."

"Honey, you can call yourself a cab if you want to," giggled the girl called Dee, "but I think 'prude' fits you a lot better." She batted her eyelashes innocently, then burst into hysterical laughter at her own joke.

Collin thought she was hilarious too. He and a few others who'd heard Dee's remark held their sides and hee-hawed at Andy's expense.

Andy didn't acknowledge that she'd even heard what Dee said. She pulled her arm out of Collin's grasp, stood up, and began to walk away. She'd gone only a few steps when she felt his hand grip her arm once more. This time his hold on her was so fierce it hurt. He yanked her backward, pulling her off balance, and she fell into her chair with a jarring thud.

"I said . . . *we* aren't ready to go, yet. I'll tell you when you're leaving." Each time she tried to stand up, he pulled her down again. They were becoming the center of attention. And as much as Collin and his friends were enjoying his little game, she didn't find it humorous at all. She hated scenes, but she was prepared to make one if Collin didn't let her go.

Using all her strength to resist Collin's tugging, she shoved back at him with all her might. She caught him unprepared and knocked him sideways into Dee. To keep from falling he had to release her arm, and she bolted and ran for the saloon's double doors. Once across the open space of the dance floor, she had to skirt tables so tightly crowded together she was forced to squeeze through sideways. She dodged waitresses with loaded trays and ducked past several rowdy customers, some of whom called out to her as she quickly scurried past them.

"She's gettin' away, kid."

"You're some spitfire, honey. How about. . . ."

"Git that there little dogie, cowboy."

She didn't have to look behind her; she sensed that Collin was right on her heels. She was determined to reach the door before he could reach her. She was almost there. With a final lunge she tried for her one avenue of escape, the doors.

She wasn't fast enough. She felt his steel grip banding her wrist. He was forcing her to stand and fight, and she was fully prepared to do battle if it was necessary. If he wanted another scene, he'd get a doozy. "Collin Ellis, let go. . . ."

Suddenly, the air hissed out of him like a deflated balloon, and Collin sank to the floor at her feet. She was totally bewildered as she stared at him sitting there, surprise written all over his face, rubbing his chin. Had she done that? She was plenty mad, but she didn't remember hitting him.

"Let's go, Andy," said an angry and determined voice next to her. "Don't bother to thank Mr. Ellis for a lovely evening. I think I already did."

"Joe! What are you doing . . . ?" Where had he materialized from? How long had he been there, watching her be humiliated?

One look at Joe's face cut off any questions she might have asked. This was the time to move, not talk. As a crowd began to form around them, Joe led her out of the John Starr Saloon.

She walked across the parking lot beside him, as docile as a kitten. And when he yanked open the door on the passenger side of his old Chevy, she got in without a word. The door on the driver's side was stuck, and it took her pushing and his pulling to get it open. Moments later they pulled out of the parking lot and into the late-night Santa Monica traffic.

"Where are you taking . . . ?" began Andy, but the angry sparks from his furious blue eyes silenced her. He glared at her for a long second, then turned back to the road to concentrate on his driving.

It really doesn't matter where we're going, she thought, as long as it's far away from the John Starr Saloon and the charming and very well-bred Collin Ellis. Morgana Crane was only slightly worse at judging a person's character than she was.

She stared out the window at the flickering lights that blinked at her out of the darkness. She shivered, and her skin felt clammy as the events of her miserable evening were replayed in her mind. She leaned her head back against the leather seat and closed her eyes. She was glad Joe didn't want to talk. Suddenly her head hurt, and she appreciated the quiet, which was only slighty interrupted by the chug-chugging of the car's laboring old engine.

Slowly she realized the engine was no longer chugging. They'd stopped, but she was reluctant to open her eyes. She had no desire to face the irate Joe Duffy and his accusing, penetrating looks. She couldn't pretend to be asleep forever. Tentatively lifting one quivering eyelid, she peeked at him. He'd brought her home.

Joe sat with his back to his door, staring at her intently. His lips were pressed together tightly, grim and unsmiling. Only his eyes blazed with the questions she knew she would have to answer. She didn't know where to start. She remembered something Big Andy liked to say when the Raiders, his favorite team, were piling up yardage. Something about the best defense being a good offense. Well, here goes nothing, she thought, and bravely plunged ahead.

"What were you doing at the John Starr?" she demanded.

"Isn't that supposed to be my question, Andy? It just so happens I went there looking for you."

"Looking for me? But how did you know I'd be there? I didn't even know it until we pulled in to park."

"I was at the skating rink," said Joe. "I got there just after you left. I asked Liz to skate, and she told me what had happened when you and Collin were there. She was pretty mad about the cold shoulder he gave her and Gabby. But she said it all worked out 'in the end.' Seeing a pompous snob like Collin fall flat on his big fat personality made putting up with his rudeness worthwhile. Those were her words, not mine. She also said he was so totally embarrassed and outraged when Tonio tried to pick him up off the floor that he barely stopped to take off his skates before dragging you away."

"But I didn't tell Liz where we were going. How did she know?"

"She didn't. I asked her, but she said he pulled you out of there so fast she didn't get a chance to talk to you. So I guessed—and I was right."

"Why the John Starr? It would've been the last place I'd have expected to find me."

"But not Ellis. I've heard a lot of talk about that place from a couple of his cronies in the lab. I knew it was one of their favorite hangouts. I took a chance and came looking for you. As I said, it was a guess."

"A lucky guess—for me," said Andy, really meaning it.

Joe smiled at her with his eyes. "Andy, you don't belong with . . . at the John Starr. A leprechaun told me you'd be requiring some of my special, Joe Duffy-style help."

"Well, Joe Duffy, I'm very glad you came along. Your leprechaun was absolutely right. Although you have to admit I wasn't doing all that bad by myself."

"Oh, sure. You were doing great. Like a swimmer going down for the third time. Admit it, Andy Whitman. . . . You need me!" He didn't give her a chance to agree or disagree. Getting out and coming around to her side of the car, he took hold of her door handle and pulled. Her door was stuck fast.

Andy tried the handle on the inside several times, but nothing happened.

Joe motioned for her to roll down her window. Then, by wiggling the inside and the outside handles at the same time, he finally got the door to open.

"Fake door handles. What a clever trap, Mr. Duffy. I'll bet very few of your girls ever get away," teased Andy mischievously.

"No trap intended. I'm fixing up old Daisy as fast as I can. New door handles, and the gears to make them work, cost money. I never seem to have enough of that. Could you love a poor man, Andy?"

When her feet seemed to miss a step for no reason, Andy decided that one of the cracks in the path must have caught her toe. She couldn't see Joe's face in the dark, but she could feel him staring at her. She could feel him looking right into her heart. She suddenly felt a need to turn the conversation away from . . . love? Now, you're really being a silly, she told herself. She refused to feel the tingles that raced up and down her spine.

"If Collin Ellis is an example of the alternative, then give me a poor man anytime." Was that changing the subject? "I can't imagine the kind of family someone like Collin comes from." And neither can Mrs. Crane, she added silently.

"Well, my family is no mystery," said Joe. Andy could hear the pride in his voice. She had changed the subject at last. "I think it's the most wonderful family in the whole world."

"Are there a lot of Duffys?"

"That depends on whom you ask. I think there are just enough of us—ten."

"*Ten!* You're so lucky. I would love to have a lot of sisters and brothers."

"You say that because you never had to wait two hours in line to use the bathroom. I've got five sisters. John and Jamey aren't too bad. But Colleen, Corrine, Megan, Matty, and Molly could drive you to distraction. I'm surprised the lot of us haven't made Mom and Pop bananas."

"John, Jamey, Corrine, Molly?"

"Overwhelming, aren't we?"

"Phew—ten Duffys," gasped Andy.

"Actually there're hundreds more. Ten Duffys were all that could fit in our house. But there're Grandma and Grandpa Duffy, Uncle Wyllam, Uncle Sean, Aunt Maggie, Cousin Ian, Cousin Brian. . . ." In the faint yellow glow of the porch light, Andy watched his smile widen into an oversized grin.

"I wish I had a big family. Dad and I only have each other. Well, I do have an Uncle Steve in Lexington, Michigan; he's a confirmed bachelor. And two maiden aunts in Tarrytown, New York. Aunt Lois and Aunt Brenda are my mom's older sisters. But here in California, there's just Big Andy and me; my mom's been dead for almost four years. Two Whitmans compared to all those Duffys; we're not much in the way of a family, are we?"

"You could always become a Duffy. Anyway, head counts aren't what's important; it's whether you feel like a family or not."

Andy let the becoming-a-Duffy part slip by without comment. "We do. Big Andy and Little Andy—we're a team."

"I think your dad's a great guy."

"You do? You know my dad?"

"I . . . um . . . mean, well, he's got to be a great guy, doesn't he? After all, he is your father—and look at you." He looked at her and looked at her. Neither of them said anything. And Andy looked back for what seemed like hours instead of minutes. "I guess you'd better go in," he said finally.

"I guess."

"Well, good night, then," he said softly. He seemed as truly reluctant as she was to dispel the mood that surrounded them. "I guess I'll be seeing you, Handy Andy." He tapped the tip of her nose with a finger and started down the short cement walk to his car.

"I guess," Andy whispered. She watched him go, feeling sadly disappointed. One minute she'd thought he was going to. . . . And then he was gone. She didn't know what to think. Very strange, she thought. Joe Duffy was a very strange guy. She shook her head in confusion; she was feeling a little strange, too. She went into her house and shut the door, locking it behind her.

"Andy?"

"Dad? Are you still up? Waiting for your little girl to come home safely?"

"As usual."

"I wish you wouldn't worry so much; you don't have to. Promise me you won't wait up anymore. I know you have to go in early tomorrow."

"Umm? Sorry, no promises. And it's not so very late. In fact, you're home a little early, aren't you?" Big Andy examined his watch through squinting eyes. "It's barely after eleven."

"I was tired, I guess."

"Was that Collin who drove away? He must have had his engine overhauled since he roared through here at seven-thirty."

"No, that wasn't Collin's car. That was Joe Duffy. I know him from the hospital. He drove me home."

"Oh, he did? Joe Duffy's a nice boy."

"And how would you know that, Dad? Have you ever met Joe?"

"Might be. I go a lot of places and meet a lot of people. A few of them have been Duffys."

Andy remembered all the Duffys Joe had told her were in his family. It was very possible for her dad to know a Duffy or two. There had to be millions of them.

"Besides, he has to be nice; he's your friend, isn't he?"

Well, answer him, Andy. Is he—or isn't he? She stared at her dad in silence.

9

One Bright Idea

JASON TOOK HIS last shaky step off the exercise ramp to the cheers and applause of Andy and the elated physical therapist, Dave Mayer. For many weeks Andy had been accompanying Jason down to physical therapy. She knew how difficult each long hour of grueling work had been for him. The valiant struggle he'd made daily, adjusting to his new leg, often left him in a state of total exhaustion. She'd seen the tears of pain in his eyes, and she understood the immense amount of courage it took for him to endure that pain, time after time. But for Andy, it had been a rare opportunity to see beneath the tough, often cruel, exterior that Jason showed to most of the world. With all her heart, she sympathized with the child's feelings of injustice. His was an overwhelming burden of hurt and anguish. She'd been there to hold him when he cried. She'd soothed him when he hurt. She'd encouraged him when he failed. And now she celebrated with him—his success.

Jason had begun therapy reluctantly. He didn't want an artificial leg; he wanted his own leg back. He was angry. But more than that, he was terrified of what lay ahead. At first he wouldn't go to the therapy room. Then he agreed to go, but only if Andy went with him. Andy believed he really did need her, and she'd been able to convince her supervisor that she would be able to help Jason in ways the regular therapist couldn't. And she'd been right; today proved it.

Jason was walking on his new leg. And all the painful, hurting steps he'd had to take to get there, he had taken for Andy. Because she asked him over and over again to try—for her. Because she loved him, even when he was acting his most unlovable. For her he tried again. Again, and again, and again.

In return for what Andy considered so little to give where a child's life was concerned, she received so much. She saw the gradual change in Jason's interaction with the other children. He showed a genuine concern for the playmates he'd so often shunned. A kind of an understanding and friendship had even seemed to grow between Jason and Eric, before Eric went home with his light casts and crutches. Most surprising of all was the bond of love that Jason and Robbie Washington shared. They seemed to give each other something that went beyond friendship. Robbie adored Jason. And Jason couldn't have been more protective or loving to his constant shadow had Robbie been his own little brother. Andy was beginning to discover so many of the real rewards her career in nursing would bring her.

In a swaying, uneven gait, Jason made his way slowly toward Andy's outstretched arms. "I'm not so good at this yet, but in a few more weeks, Andy, I'm going to be able to run to you. Fast, too. You'll see." Jason's words came out as gasps from the effort of each small step.

"You'll be running, all right," said Dr. Silverstein. She'd entered the therapy room unnoticed and stood beside Dave, the therapist. "But, as of Tuesday, young man, you'll be doing your walking—and running—at home." Dr. Silverstein was Jason's surgeon. She'd already told Andy how pleased she was with Jason's recovery. Since Andy'd become involved in his therapy program, Jason had progressed much faster than she had dared hope.

Jason looked from Dr. Silverstein to Andy. Two huge tears slipped down his pale cheeks. "No! No—no—no. I can't go home. I can't walk without Andy."

"Come on, Jase. That's silly. You know you can. You can walk anyplace. It's just like in the hospital," insisted Dave. "You've proved it. You can do anything, man."

"Dave's right, Jason. You don't need me anymore. You'll be running in no time at all," agreed Andy.

"No, I won't. I won't ever run. I won't walk anymore. Not ever!"

"Perhaps you should take Jason back to his room, Andrea," suggested the doctor.

"Could we just have a minute together, alone? I think Jason and I should have a little talk," said Andy.

Dr. Silverstein went to Jason and reached out her hand.

Gasping for breath, tears streaming down his face, frantically clinging to Andy with his thin little arms, Jason shook his head. He wasn't going home. And he wasn't letting go of Andy, either.

Andy sat down on a chair and pulled Jason down onto her lap. "Jason? Why don't you want to go home? Please, will you tell me?" she asked in a soft voice.

He didn't answer. Hesitantly he nodded.

Dr. Silverstein smiled at Andy. She turned and left the therapy room, and Dave followed.

"I can't walk without you, Andy. It hurts too much when you aren't there," Jason sniffled.

With one of the tissues she always kept in her uniform pocket, she wiped his eyes. She waited while he blew his nose. "You know the pain is going away; every day it hurts less. It doesn't hurt as much now as it did when you started coming to therapy, does it?"

"It stopped hurting when you came with me. I don't want to go home. I'll fall down."

"But you fall down here. Falling down, Jason? Is that what's bothering you? You fall down even when I'm helping you."

"But you don't laugh. If I fall down at home, people will laugh at me. They'll call me a baby—who can't even walk yet. I'm not a baby, am I, Andy? I'm not."

"Of course you're not. I happen to know that Jason Fox is a very brave boy. It takes a lot of courage to learn to walk on a new leg. And it takes a lot of courage to risk falling down and then to get up and start all over again. But I think it would take an extra-brave young man with a special kind of courage to keep on trying even if people did laugh at him. Are you brave enough to do that, Jason? Do you have special courage?''

"Maybe. But I would for sure if you were there. I want to keep doing my exercises with you . . . here.''

"You will be doing them here with me—some of the time. When you go home that doesn't mean we won't see each other anymore, you know. You can't get rid of me that easily, kiddo. You still have to come back to the hospital for therapy with Dave. And I'll come and work with you just as I always have.''

"Will you really?'' His teary eyes lit up.

"You'd better believe it. We'll get to see each other at least two times a week. The only difference will be that you'll live at home with your family. They love you, Jason, and miss you very much. You'll be an outpatient at the hospital. You'll get to see so much of me and this therapy room that you'll skip walking and go right for running—just so you won't have to come here anymore,'' teased Andy.

"No, I won't. Then I'll come back and help other kids learn to walk on their profeetis.'' He was smiling at last.

"*Prosthesis,* Jason. And I'll just bet you will, too. Come on,'' Andy said, getting up and helping Jason to stand. "You hop into that wheelchair and let me give you my A-number-one, special first-class super-duper-express, look-ma-no-hands ride back to pediatrics.'' Jason let her help him into the chair and adjust his artificial leg on the foot rest. "Hang on, kiddo. Here we go.''

Andy and Jason's sound effects made the wheelchair ride to the third floor seem far more dangerous and exciting than it actually was. The elevator passengers kept looking around the car to see where the sound came from as Jason sat in his chair and revved up his engine without moving his lips. Everyone gave everyone else the strangest and most confused looks. Andy tried to maintain a blank look of innocence. When they left the elevator car at pedi-3, both she and Jason were overcome with gales of laughter. They were still laughing as she pushed him past the floor desk where Dr. Silverstein was having a quiet conversation with Mrs. Wernick.

The doctor looked up at Andy questioningly.

Andy smiled broadly, nodding in an unspoken answer.

Then Dr. Silverstein acknowledged Andy's success with a high sign and a "well-done!" smile.

When she entered the ward, Andy wasn't surprised to see Robbie sitting patiently on the foot of Jason's bed. Lately Robbie seemed to spend much more time in ward five or on the sunny play patio with Jason than he did in his own semiprivate room. The friendship had started with Robbie's loneliness for Heather when she was placed in intensive care for several days. But now he came because of the special closeness that had developed between the adoring little boy and his older friend.

"Can you play now, Jason?" asked Robbie crawling off his bed.

"Sure. Know what? I walked great today, didn't I, Andy?"

She nodded in agreement as she helped Jason remove his leg and slip into bed.

"You want to color? I brought my best book. It's new—about rodeo things. And I got new crayons, too." Robbie proudly held out the coloring book and his shoe box full of bright new crayons.

"Yeah? Let me see your new book. Gee, Rob. This is neat. I really like it. Did your mom and dad give it to you?"

Robbie shook his head. "Joe did. He said I was the best boy he ever took blood from. I had a whole bunch of tests, and I didn't even move once. Drakala took all my blood out."

"Not all of it, I hope," laughed Andy. She was surprised to find that she enjoyed Robbie's enthusiastic chatter about Joe.

"Can I color this one?" Jason pointed to a picture of a bucking bronco that had tossed its rider into the air. "You're lucky, Rob. This is a great coloring book."

"You can do any picture. That's a good one, huh?" Robbie climbed back up onto the end of Jason's bed, being careful not to land on top of his friend. Robbie had never asked Jason about his missing leg. That was just how Jason was; and Robbie accepted it.

"Today was Jason's lucky day, too. Wasn't it, Jason?" Andy wanted to reinforce the positive feelings he was beginning to have about going home.

"Did Joe give you a surprise for being the best, too?"

"Nope. But I'm walking so great on my new leg that Dr. Silverstein said I could go home on Tuesday."

Suddenly Robbie's shoe box hit the floor. Crayons scattered and rolled in every direction. "I don't want you to go."

Oh, no! What have I done now? thought Andy. She watched Robbie's face crumple as the tears welled up in his big, sad eyes. She just wasn't thinking. She should have known how Robbie would feel about Jason going home.

Jason took Robbie's hand and held it. "Why are you crying, Rob? Aren't you glad I can walk as good as anybody?"

Robbie wiped his tears on his pajama sleeve. "But you're my best friend. I don't want you to go away without me. You promised to be my friend forever. You promised."

"I still will be. I still promise. I'll come back to the hospital a lot. Won't I, Andy? I'm going to be a therapy-on-the-outside patient, aren't I?"

Andy nodded. She was proud of the mixed-up way Jason was explaining to his friend what she'd just explained to him.

"But I never had a best friend before. Except maybe Heather. But she's a girl and she doesn't count. Not like you do. All the other kids laugh at me. They call me a little baby and say I get fits. They don't want to play with me. Please, Jason. Can I go home with you? You said you'd teach me to walk on your pretend leg. You said!"

Andy couldn't believe what she was hearing. How could anyone be so cruel? "Robbie, what children said you were a baby? Who told you that you had 'fits'?"

Robbie looked down at his teddy-bear slippers. Andy could tell he was not going to answer her question.

"I guess I said it," whispered Jason. He looked ashamed. "But that was before Robbie was my friend. When I said that, I hated everybody, especially Eric. I don't say it anymore. Robbie and I are really friends now. Honest."

"Best friends," the littler boy reminded him. "Will you really come back to see me? What if I'm not here? What if I have to go home?" A new round of tears seemed to threaten.

"I'll bet my mom will drive me over to your house to visit. And your mom can drive you over to see me, too," suggested Jason.

"With your pretend leg you could even walk to my house, huh? You could, couldn't you, Jason?"

"Sure, I could. Maybe even run there."

It was obvious to Andy that, in Robbie's eyes, Jason was bigger and stronger and better than Superman. He could do anything. He was Robbie's superhero. But it was just as clear that Jason returned Robbie's love, that he needed the younger boy to look up to him, and that they were very good for each other. She would speak to their parents, she decided, and see if she couldn't help the boys get together after they left the hospital.

"Okay, fellas, it's time for Jason to take his rest. He had a rough workout today, Robbie. Why don't you leave your new coloring book on his tray? Let's gather up all the crayons and put them back into your box and leave them on the tray, too. Then, after Jason has rested, you can come back here, or take everything onto the play patio and color. Okay?"

"Uh-huh," agreed Robbie.

"Thanks, Rob. I'll take a real quick rest," yawned Jason.

Without warning Robbie leaned over and planted a noisy kiss on Jason's cheek. Then he scampered down from the bed and raced off to his own room.

A very surprised Jason just sat there, fingers touching his kissed cheek, while Andy fluffed his pillows and straightened his covers. Then she, too, kissed the boy—the new Jason Fox—the boy she'd come to love just as much as Robbie had. She bent down and gently touched a fingertip to each of his drooping eyelids.

Jason gave her a drowsy smile, but quickly replaced it with a huge yawn. Then he snuggled down under his blankets to rest.

After tucking Jason in, Andy went off in search of Curious Robbie, in case he'd decided to go to his room by way of the pony rides again. She was relieved to find him with Heather and Sammy, the ulcer patient from ward five, sitting on the end of Heather's bed. The bed was covered with storybooks, but the children seemed far more engrossed in their conversation than they were in looking at the pictures.

Andy stopped to hear what they talked so seriously about. Not again! she thought. This hospital is having an epidemic of children not wanting to go home, today. This time it was Heather who was refusing to leave the hospital.

"I don't care what Jason says. I don't ever want to go home. I think the hospital is the best place to live," Heather confided to the two little boys who sat on her bed. "I like to be sick."

"I guess it's okay," agreed Sammy. He sounded uncertain. "But I like my house too."

"When I go home, Jason is going to come to my house. So I don't mind if I get all better," explained Robbie.

"I hope I never get better. Then I can live here forever," said Heather.

As if a light had suddenly flashed on in Andy's head, she understood: Heather was afraid to go home, afraid of her mother. There'd been no further episodes like the one after the child's surgery. But Andy knew that had been only one of many terrible explosions for Mrs. Berk. How could Heather forget years of having to live in constant fear that she could never be good enough or quiet enough or lovable enough to please her mother? Mrs. Berk had to get professional help so things could change. And it would take Heather a long time to forget all the ugliness that had happened to her. Yet, the situation didn't seem as hopeless as it once had. Andy remembered the day she'd found Mrs. Berk with Heather; she trembled from the terrible memory. It wasn't something one could easily put out of mind. She could understand why Heather would want to stay at Bayshore Medical Center; it was the only place she'd ever felt really safe.

"You might decide to change your mind about going home someday, Heather," said Andy, joining the children. She knew that a decision would be made shortly as to whether the little girl would go home with her mother or be put into a temporary home. Mrs. Berk needed counseling; Andy hoped any decisions about Heather's life and welfare would be left in the hands of experts.

"No, I won't," insisted Heather.

93

"I think that's dumb," announced Sammy. "You can't stay here forever. Your mommy will get mad if you don't ever come home. I'd miss my mommy and daddy too much."

"I don't miss anybody. I like it here. Will my mommy get mad because I don't want to go home, Andy? Don't tell her. Please don't tell her," Heather pleaded.

"You know I'd never do that, Heather. I promise. Now, let's forget all about mommies and going home. Let's do something fun. Would you like to—"

Robbie interrupted Andy's question. "I know why she likes it here so much. Heather has the best bed."

"Oh, Robbie, every bed is exactly the same, and you know it. Now you quit your teasing," said Andy.

"No, sir. She's got a window. She can see out. I like Heather's bed, and I hate mine. I'm not going to sleep in it, and I'm not going to have it anymore. I'm going home with Jason."

"I'm afraid you can't do that, honey," Andy told him.

"Then I'll run away. I want to have a bed by the window. I want to see good stuff, too. Not just nothing!"

"Yeah. And me too," seconded Sammy.

Andy sat down on Heather's bed and looked out the window. Robbie had a point, she decided. She *could* see a lot of good stuff down there. Robbie should be able to see it, too. All the children should. From his bed Robbie could only see out the top of the window. His view was of sky and clouds. It was nice, but not as nice as what she was looking at now. Heather's view was of the entire Bayshore Marina. She could see people and beach and soaring seabirds. Below her was Sea Cove Landing with its glorious blue water and colorful sailboats. This view should be shared by all the children—not just those with beds by the window.

"You know something, Robbie Washington? I think you're absolutely right. You do deserve a 'best' bed just like Heather's. All the kids in this hospital do."

"Are you going to give Robbie my bed?" asked Heather, her lower lip pouting out with concern.

94

"No, I wouldn't do that. But I may be able to give Robbie a wonderful surprise."

"What, Andy? What?" cried Robbie eagerly.

"Tell us what," echoed Sammy.

"Not just yet, kids. You'll have to give me a little time to work this out. But have I got an idea!"

Andy finally found Mrs. Grymes in the nurses' lounge; she tried not to stare, but she couldn't help herself. This was one of the few times she'd ever seen her supervisor looking so unnurselike—sitting in the big chair, white cap lying in her lap, feet up, and shoes off. She never could have imagined such an unusual picture—Mrs. Grymes at rest. Andy would have sworn that the dauntless Simon LeGrymes never needed to rest. And certainly she never needed to remove her sensible shoes while she was on duty; her feet wouldn't dare hurt her.

"Excuse me, Mrs. Grymes. I don't want to bother you, but—"

"No, no. Come in, Andrea. Just taking a short break. What is it?" Her supervisor might have seemed completely exhausted when Andy opened the door, but as soon as she stepped into the lounge Mrs. Grymes sat bolt upright—alert and menacing as ever.

"I . . . um, well . . . I . . . ." What *are* you doing here? she asked herself. Are you crazy? Andrea Leigh Whitman, why are you asking for trouble? A picture of Robbie's little face, his sad, trusting eyes filled with disappointment, floated before her. That's why, she told herself. You're here for the children.

"What is it, Andrea? Is there a problem on the floor? One of the children?"

"Oh, no, nothing like that. Except . . . well, maybe . . . yes."

"For heaven's sake, child, which is it? Yes, no, or maybe?"

"It's yes. Definitely yes," Andy said adamantly.

"Sit down, Andrea. We'd better talk about it," said Mrs. Grymes. She patted the footstool her feet rested on, but she didn't remove them, just moved them over a little bit.

She must be wiped out, thought Andy. What a pleasant change. The brief feeling of understanding that passed over her truly surprised Andy. And she prayed that a Mrs. Grymes with her feet up was a Mrs. Grymes with her guard down.

"Andrea? What is this 'yes, definitely' problem of yours?"

"Room four. Actually it's the window in room four. Well, the window and the bed. And Robbie Washington."

"Robbie Washington threw his bed out the window of room four? Andrea, you know you're not making a lot of sense. What about Robbie, his bed, and the window? I'm not in the mood for silly student-nurse jokes."

"No. Yes. I can explain. Heather—"

"Heather? Not Robbie?"

"Well, both actually. You see, the problem is really with Heather's bed. It's next to the window. When she sits up she can see the marina, Sea Cove Landing, and the beach."

"Yes, I know. And . . . ?"

"And Robbie can't see anything from his bed except some sky and a few clouds. He feels cheated—and I don't blame him. I took a good look out of Heather's window and the view is absolutely beautiful. Robbie's missing the people, the sailboats, the sea gulls, everything. He's so upset about it, he's threatening to run away."

"Somehow that doesn't really surprise me. Running away is miniature Mr. Washington's favorite pastime." The corners of Mrs. Grymes's mouth seemed to turn down as she spoke about Robbie.

"Oh. I didn't think you. . . ."

"Knew? It's my business to know what happens on this floor. And he's taken off on days you weren't here, too, dear. When he does, most of my girls holler out for help. Some of them aren't as resourceful as others. I've chased that little maverick around pedi-3 a few times myself.

"Even though I can sympathize with his desire for a view, and with his complaint, there is room for only one bed by the window. Perhaps we can move him into Heather's bed when she leaves, if he's still here."

"Couldn't we make a view for him too?"

"How would you go about doing that? The hospital has strict rules about nurses-in-training cutting windows into the walls."

"We would paint a view for Robbie. We could paint a view for every child in pediatrics—in every room. But we could start with room four. Do you think the hospital has any rules about N.I.T.s painting the walls?" Andy was so excited about her idea she forgot to be afraid. She just blurted it out. She felt like grabbing her supervisor's hand and getting on bended knee to beg her. She'd do anything she could to make her say it was okay to paint the walls in room four.

"I don't know. I'm not sure," mumbled Mrs. Grymes as she considered Andy's proposal.

Andy was not about to accept any answer but the one she had to hear. She stood up and paced the floor of the lounge as she talked. "We could use the long wall across from Robbie's bed. You have to admit it's an awfully monotonous beige. That's hardly conducive to making a child feel better and want to get well faster. Anything would be better than plain beige, right? But with an ocean, waves, fish, birds, boats, sky, sunshine, and clouds . . . can't you just see it? It could be spectacular. It could, couldn't it?" Finally running out of breath, Andy stopped talking.

"Yes, I suppose it could. But who is the Rembrandt who's going to do all this artwork on the hospital walls—for free?"

"Me. I can paint. I even wanted to be an artist once. And I have a lot of friends who are terrific artists. Liz Jones, in emergency, was in design before she decided to become a nurse. Really, Mrs. Grymes, I'd love to do it, and I know my friends would help," exclaimed Andy. "I'd paint it on my day off."

"Your intentions are good, Andrea, but not very practical. That's a lot of wall in room four. Multiply it by all the rooms on pedi-3 and you have a new lifetime career on your hands. It will cut into your nursing a bit, don't you think?" Mrs. Grymes cast a skeptical look at Andy.

"We'll get it all done in one day. I promise. I'll get everybody to help. I won't even start until I have a full crew of painters lined up. Please, Mrs. Grymes? Won't you help me get permission to start? Right away?"

"I guess I could speak to Dr. Stewart; he is rather friendly with

Mr. Pippin, the chairman of the hospital board. But I doubt that the board would agree to take on any unnecessary expenditure."

"We could—I mean, I could ask for donations. Not just money, but paint and stuff like that. What if I promise the whole job won't cost the hospital a cent?"

"I'd say we—I mean, you might stand a chance."

"Okay!" Andy grabbed her supervisor out of her chair, stocking feet and all, and danced her in a circle. "Thank you. Thank you. It'll be wonderful. You're going to love it. And you can help, too. Oh, thank you so much."

"I intended to help." Mrs. Grymes tactfully untangled herself from Andy's impulsive grip. "I know better than to let you and your friends go off on a painting lark without any kind of intelligent supervision." This Mrs. Grymes, muttering her thoughts aloud, was at least a million miles away from Simon LeGrymes: "Let's see. Talk to Dr. Stewart. Arrange a new room for Robbie and Heather for, um . . . two days. *Oh!* Andrea?"

"Yes, Mrs. Grymes?" Bursting with happy excitement at her supervisor's enthusiasm, Andy was already starting for the door to spread her good news to the other nurses.

"Start organizing your painting people," Mrs. Grymes said, putting on her shoes. "It's not too early to be looking around for those donations you think will be so easily gotten. Keep me informed of your progress." The supervisor straightened her uniform and pinned her cap on. "I'd better wash out my old overalls."

Andy wanted to shout hurrahs, turn somersaults, throw her arms around Mrs. Grymes's neck, and give her a big, fat kiss. That's what she wanted to do. But, walking sedately behind her muttering supervisor, and grinning as if she'd just won Irish Sweepstakes is what she did instead.

10

The Nosey Joe Mistake

I FEEL AS though I'd just been through the longest day of my entire life, thought Andy. She rummaged through her locker until she located the errant brush she kept there. She found herself sighing with each stroke the brush made through her tangled brown curls. "I feel a hundred years old," she sadly informed the weary reflection that looked back at her from mirror inside the locker door. "But you, poor dear, look it." Her usually pert smile seemed to drop from the corners of her mouth. The sparkling green eyes she considered her best feature were the same dull camouflage green of the old army tank her dad had driven twenty-five years ago in the army reserve. In fact, she decided, leaning in for a closer inspection, a strategic battle seemed to be taking place in her hair that very minute. "You're a real mess, Andrea Leigh Whitman. You know that?" The image acknowledged its agreement with a curt nod. Giving up on her hair, she threw her brush into the locker, pulled out her sweater, and slammed the door shut. She was just too tired to care how she appeared to the rest of the world. Her arms felt like lead weights as she pushed them through her sweater sleeves, and her fingers had no patience with the small buttons that no longer fit their holes. With a sigh, she looked over at the stack of books waiting on the green couch for her to lug home. It just wasn't fair. On top of everything else, she was loaded with homework.

At first she recognized only one of the voices. It was Dr. Dan, and he was having a heated argument with a woman. She didn't recognize the woman's voice, but she was sure it wasn't Mrs. Grymes. She'd seen her supervisor leave the hospital hours ago. Could it be Heather's mother? "Oh, heavens, I hope not," she whispered.

Deciding to leave her books on the couch, she walked to the door. At least, she thought, I should let them know they're being overheard. I'd die if they walked in here and thought I was eavesdropping. Quietly she opened the door and stuck out her head.

She was right about it being Dr. Dan, but the woman Andy found herself nose to nose with was Mrs. Stewart. She and the doctor were yelling at each other in loud, angry voices. Andy's head was right in the middle of their furious debate.

"Yes, Andréa?" asked the doctor, directing at Andy several of the visual arrows he'd been aiming at his wife.

"I—Oh, I'm—I'm so sorry. I was just listening—I mean, I wasn't actually listening. I thought you might want help, Doctor. In case she was getting hysterical again. But I didn't know it was your wife you were fighting with. I have to go now. Please excuse me, Doctor, Mrs. Stewart." Andy ran for the closing elevator doors and leaped through just as they were sliding shut. The back of her sweater was caught between them, but with a sharp tug she pulled it free. If there had not already been several other passengers in the car, she would have banged her head on the back wall as her sweater, with her in it, came loose.

She refused to look at any of them, but she knew they were staring at her. Her face aflame, she studied the scuffed toes of her sensible shoes. Nurses do not leap into elevators—especially if the doors are nearly closed. Frogs leap; N.I.T.s do not, she told herself. She felt like a fool. Heaven forbid if Mrs. Grymes had been there to see her. Thank goodness she'd already gone.

The person standing next to Andy snickered.

She looked up and, pretending indifference, concentrated on the blinking floor numbers overhead. Silently she prayed for the red L to light.

"Outsiders rarely like the things they overhear during a family quarrel," whispered the snickerer.

She didn't have to look at him to know who it was. Joe—the old Joe. The smart-alecky, wisecracking, always-making-her-feel-like-a-fool Joe. She'd hoped, after the incident at the John Starr, that he'd act differently and give up his teasing. Obviously she'd been mistaken—about a lot of things. And she was in no mood for his warped sense of humor tonight. He had absolutely no idea what had happened, and he'd jumped to some pretty ugly conclusions. *He* was calling her an eavesdropper! Joe Duffy, who didn't know the very first thing about minding his own business!

The minute the elevator had reached the lobby and the doors had opened wide enough for her to escape, Andy was through them and running for the parking lot. She didn't bother to look behind her to see if he was following. She ran as fast as she could, up one row of cars and down another, searching for Jackee's yellow bug.

"Why all the panic? You look as if the devil himself is after you," called Liz, watching Andy run toward her.

Liz was leaning on the VW, her long legs crossed at the ankles, looking very relaxed in spite of the rumpled uniform, which testified that she, too, had just come off duty.

To Andy, in her frazzled state, Liz looked like a sleek, bronze Siamese cat who'd spent the day lazing in the sun. She couldn't remember ever seeing Liz out of breath, ruffled, or panicky. Andy knew she must make a ridiculous picture tearing around the parking lot in a flap.

"I've never been so embarrassed in my life," gasped Andy. She found a spot to lean on and tried to catch her breath. "I don't even want to talk about it!"

"*I've never been so embarrassed; I don't even want to talk about it?* You can't do that to me. Unless you want to be responsible for killing a nurse, you'd better talk! You've got me dying of curiosity."

Andy was too humiliated to admit what kind of a fool she'd just made out of herself in front of Dr. Dan and his wife, not to mention an elevator packed with gawking strangers—and mean, miserable

101

Joe Duffy. Enough people knew already. "Please, Liz? Not now. I really can't talk about it. Call me tonight and we'll talk then. And please don't say anything in front of the others. Okay?" Her pulse was returning to normal, and her heart no longer pounded to be let out of her chest. She was able to breathe again.

Liz was a good friend. Andy smiled at her for understanding and for letting the subject drop. All of Andy's friends were very special.

"Now, how can I talk about *it* if I don't know what *it* is? Right? Let's change the subject. Let's talk about something trivial, of major unimportance, something of no value whatsoever."

"And what would that be?" asked Andy.

"Why, homework, of course." Liz made Andy laugh. "No, seriously, I need to get our anatomy assignment from you. I can't find my assignment book anywhere. *Again.*"

"I think you lose it on purpose, hoping I won't know it either. But you're out of luck, Lizzie. I have it right here in my note—Oh, no! Not that, too?" Andy felt like collapsing to the pavement and shedding a few hard-earned tears.

"Now what? Or can't I ask?"

"I left all my books up in the nurses' lounge. And my class notes. And my purse. Everything."

"No big deal. We've got plenty of time. Come on, I'll walk you back to get them," offered Liz, taking a few steps away from the car.

"*No!*" Andy shouted, grabbing Liz by the arm. "Really. No thanks." She lowered her voice about ten octaves; she'd given Liz quite a start. "I don't need them; I did all tomorrow's work at lunch. My purse is empty, except for a lipstick and a toothless comb. Who'd steal that? It didn't have a dime in it," she explained quickly.

"Are you sure? I don't mind walking back." Liz looked baffled at her friend's nervous behavior.

"Yes. Honestly. I'm positive. Can you get the assignment from someone else? I can't remember what it was. I'm sorry."

"Oooh, don't be sorry. You've given me the excuse I need to call Jonny or Todd or Alexander or Jonah or. . . ."

"Are all those guys in *our* anatomy class?"

"Dear, dear Andy, don't be silly. Of course they're not. But they might know someone who is," laughed Liz.

"I have the phone numbers at home of some N.I.T.s who *are* in our class. So if your method of getting the assignment doesn't work, I can give them to you when you call."

"I may not get the anatomy assignment by calling up all those delicious males, but I'll bet I can line up an anatomy lesson for this coming Saturday night." Liz had done it again. Both girls were laughing, and Andy felt better already.

"At last. There they are. Jackee, Monica, step it up, will you? Patches is waiting," shouted Liz. "I could've walked by now."

"Your dog is waiting?" Andy looked into the VW. "Where?"

"At the vet's. Jackee said she'd stop there first, so I could pick him up. Then she'll drop you off and circle back this way to let Patch and me off at the Cove. My old car is at the vet's, too," explained Liz. "The mechanic doesn't give it much hope. He suggested I have it put to sleep."

"Gross joke, Liz. Very gross," complained Andy, unable to stop herself from smiling.

"Sorry we're late," Jackee apologized, glaring in Monica's direction.

"Can I help it if Mrs. Aoki was completely dilated after only three hours of labor, and little Meho chose quitting time to be born? I had to wait and see what Mrs. Aoki had, didn't I?" Monica opened her eyes wide in innocent wonder.

"And?" asked Andy.

"So? What sex *is* a Meho?" asked Liz.

"A girl. A big, beautiful, healthy girl," Monica told them proudly.

"She acts as if she personally gave birth to every baby ever born in this place. Bayshore's little mother," teased Jackee.

"You watch what you're saying, roomie. You should be grateful that talk is all I do. If they were all my babies, some of them would have to sleep in your bed," Monica retorted.

"Where? On top of the cats? Just get in the car." Jackee began to mutter under her breath, "Cats, mice, frogs, turtles, babies, what's the difference?"

Monica crawled into the back seat and gave Jackee a playful punch in the arm. "What's all this stuff doing in here again? I thought you were going to get rid of this scuba gear? Where are we supposed to sit?"

"I'm leaving it in Liz's boat locker when I drop her and Patches off. Right, Liz?" said Jackee.

"Right." Liz held the front seat forward so that Andy could follow Monica.

"Hey, wait a minute. Where is Patches going to sit?" Andy stopped hunching over and backed out of the car.

"In the back seat—with you?" whispered Liz.

"Wrong," announced Andy. "There's no way you're going to get me back there with *your* dog *and* Jack's diving getup. Monica, if you like, I'll share the front seat with you."

"No, that's all right. I don't mind Patches," answered Monica.

"Leave her back there, Andy. It'll do her good. Let her see what it's like living in a shoebox filled with wild animals," Jackee sneered gleefully. "It's my dream come true." Humming to herself she started the car.

All the way to the vet's they teased Monica good-naturedly about her babies and her growing collection of stray animals. The four girls laughed and kidded each other, and Monica got in a few good jabs at Jackee's expense, too. The jokes were just what Andy needed to keep her from thinking about her earlier embarrassing encounter with the head of pediatrics, and Joe's smart-alecky remarks.

They stopped at the vet's, and when Patches was safely packed into the tiny auto, Andy quickly discovered she was no better off sitting in the front seat than she would have been in the back. The black and white whirlwind jumped around in the back of the little VW with such abandon that he nearly tipped it over.

Jackee kept yelling at Liz to take control of the "beast who ate Tokyo" before he demolished Ms. Buggy, too.

Monica cuddled and cooed at the overexcited, rambunctious Dalmatian, which only served to encourage his unrestrained behavior.

104

Liz tried to oblige, yelling "Sit," "Stay," and "Down," but to no avail. She was finally reduced to shouting loudly, "Cut it out" and "Get off of me, you big buffalo."

Andy was kept busy dodging the Dalmatian's sloppy kisses and defending what was left of her hairstyle from his playful nips and clumsy paws.

They had to make several stops to remove the overgrown puppy from Jackee's lap, where he insisted on sitting, making it totally impossible for her to turn the steering wheel. On top of that, his licking the gear-shift knob left it too slippery for her to hold on to.

At last, the undaunted Ms. Buggy pulled into Andy's driveway over an hour and a half late.

"Hi, honey, I'm in the kitchen. You're late," called her dad, as Andy slammed the front door behind her.

"Sorry. We stopped to pick up Patches, Liz's dog, from the vet. He's really something. He turned Jackee's bug into a shambles," Andy called back, and headed for the kitchen.

"Well, don't worry. We didn't eat it all," Big Andy laughed. He met her at the kitchen door with a welcoming hug.

In return she kissed his cheek and hugged him around the middle. "Smells good. What's cooking?"

"The last of the stew you made on Sunday, a green salad, and garlic toast. Come and eat. You know—"

"Did you say *we*, Dad? Who's we?" Andy asked.

"That's what I was trying to tell you. Joe and I," answered her dad.

"Hi," Joe called from the kitchen.

Her head almost snapped off, she'd swiveled so quickly to stare at Joe. He was sitting at her kitchen table as if he actually belonged there. If Big Andy hadn't been hugging her, she'd have fallen over in surprise. "What are you doing here in my kitchen, eating my food, uninvited?" she demanded.

"Wait a minute, Andy. This is my kitchen, too, you know. And my food. And I invited Joe to stay and eat with us."

Andy knew by her dad's tone that he was upset with her. But so was she—plenty upset. How dare he? Joe Duffy, in her home, after what he'd said to her in the elevator. The gall of him! "If you invited him, Dad, then I'm sorry. But, that doesn't explain what he's doing here."

She turned to Joe. "Why did you come here? Was there something *else* you wanted to say to me? Something you forgot to mention in the elevator?" Her fierce glare never left his too-innocent face.

"On my last pickup on pedi-3, I overheard Mrs. Wernick mention that you'd left your purse and books in the nurses' lounge. She thought you might need them, so I brought them home for you. But—don't thank me. It wasn't much out of my way." Joe turned back to the half-empty bowl of stew on the table in front of him, and scooping up a big spoonful he held it out to her. "Great stew, Handy Andy. You'll make some lucky guy a wonderful wife."

"You—I—Dad, I'm not hungry. I think I'll skip dinner. I'm sorry."

"Joe, thank you for your deep, sensitive understanding and concern—for my books. I appreciate your taking the time to bring them." She spoke as icily as she could. What he didn't hear in her voice she hoped he could read in her face.

"Andy?" Her dad looked at her with such sad eyes.

The pained expression on her dad's face didn't make Andy change her mind. She knew she was disappointing him terribly. But she couldn't eat across the kitchen table from Joe; she wouldn't be able to swallow a bite of food. Her stomach felt queasy, and her head had begun to ache. Today had destroyed her nerves and severely damaged her pride. She had nothing left to fall back on. All she wanted to do was go to bed and hide. "I am really sorry, Dad. I guess I'm just too tired. Good night." She hoped her dad wouldn't be too upset, that he would understand; she was too tired to stand there another second. An eternity—with Joe sitting at the table staring at her. She ran to her bedroom and noiselessly closed the door.

Andy had no idea how long she'd been lying on her bed and shivering, even under the heavy quilt she'd pulled over her. The sound of a car engine turning over nearby jarred her back to reality. She wondered if that could be the sound of Joe's car as he drove away from her house? Her home! He had no right to come into her own home to taunt her. If it was Joe's car, the noise wasn't from her driveway. He'd been too smart to leave his old Chevy where she might see it and know he was there and not come into the house. He must have parked across the street, far enough away so she wouldn't see the Chevy when she came home. If only she had seen it. If only she had!

The tapping on her bedroom door was so faint that Andy wasn't sure she'd even heard it. But she did hear her dad calling to her softly through the closed door. For only a moment she thought of pretending to be asleep. "Yes?"

"May I come in, honey?" asked Big Andy.

"Sure, Dad." The door opened and a shaft of light from the hallway dimly illuminated her room. "Please leave the door open instead of turning on the light."

"Are you all right?" His voice held fatherly concern.

"I'm fine. I had a little headache, but it's gone now," she reassured him.

"I'm glad. Have a bad day?"

"Not the greatest, I guess." She'd made up her mind not to tell her dad what had happened on probably the worst day she'd ever had in nursing. She never lied to him, but sometimes it was better not to tell the whole story. And this was one of those times, she decided.

"I know. Joe told me some of it."

"What did Joe tell you? What did he say?" Now he'd even upset Big Andy. She could very easily learn to despise Joe Duffy.

"Not much. Just that he saw you walk, by mistake, into the middle of a very unpleasant argument between Dr. Stewart and his wife. And that they both seemed to take it out on you. He said you ran into the elevator looking extremely upset. But he thought he had something to do with your being upset, too. He'd wanted to say something to make you feel better when you got on the elevator, but he thinks he only made matters worse. He wasn't sure what he did wrong, but he knows you're upset with him. He brought your books

107

home as an excuse to come over and say he was sorry, but he left here feeling pretty low."

"When I got on the elevator, I was upset. Joe said something, and I may have misunderstood him. If I did, I'm sorry, and I'll tell him when I see him. Which I hope is. . . ." Suddenly she felt her headache coming back. Andy closed her eyes to blot out the throbbing in her head. "Dad, can't we talk about something else?"

Her dad sat down on her bed next to her and picked her up in his arms as if she were his little girl again. She felt comforted and loved and very safe.

"I think you need a woman around to talk to, Andy. I think you need a woman—like your mother." She felt his chest heave with a deep sigh. "I think we both do. It gets lonely."

Andy felt a big tear slip down her cheek. Her dad was right; they both did. They had each other, but there were still times when they both were lonely.

"You know? Maybe you should get married, have a dozen kids, and come here to live with your husband and family. With a crowd like that in this little house, who'd have time to be lonely? Besides, there'd be no room to get lonely in." She knew he was trying to cheer her up.

"What about you? Why should I do all the sacrificing? You find a nice lady, marry her, bring her home, and I'll talk to her." Hey, maybe that wasn't such a joke, after all. Big Andy did need a . . . girl friend. Four years is a long time to be alone, a long time to be a widower. He had the best part of his life still ahead of him. She'd start looking around the hospital. There might be someone there who'd be perfect for her dad.

"How about your supervisor?"

"What?" Mrs. Grymes? He couldn't be serious.

"Couldn't you talk to her if you have a problem?"

"Mrs. Grymes?" She usually is my problem, thought Andy.

"She seems like a lovely, understanding lady to me."

Andy couldn't contain the giggle that surprised her and escaped.

"You must not have met her, Dad. You can't mean Simon Le-

Grymes. Understanding? Lovely? You have to be thinking of somebody else.''

Big Andy gave her a bear hug. "Umm?"

"You don't know her the way I do, Dad. That woman's the next best thing to an ogre. She steeps N.I.T.s in boiling water to make her tea.''

"Andy, maybe you haven't given her a chance to show you how warm a person she really is. You think about it,'' Big Andy suggested, giving her an oversized grin.

"Maybe. But Mrs. Grymes a *warm* person? You know what, Dad? I happen to love you very much. Sometimes your thinking's a little weird, but you're a very nice man.'' She hugged him one last time before he stood up to leave.

After Big Andy had shut her door, Little Andy realized her headache was gone.

11

Joe to the Roundup

TWO DAYS HAD passed since Andy had presented her exciting idea to Mrs. Grymes. And, although it seemed to Andy that Mrs. Grymes had forgotten all about it, Robbie certainly hadn't. Every time she walked into his room, he asked about his surprise. What was it? When would he get it? Andy felt like the poor woman in the commercial whose whole family keeps asking, "Is it soup yet?"

"It'll be soup when Mrs. Grymes says it's soup," snapped Andy. Then she was sorry she'd lost her temper. For a small child, an hour is as long as a day when you're waiting for something special.

"Huh?" asked Robbie, confused by Andy's answer.

"Curious Robbie, you'll just have to be patient."

"I been patient, Andy."

"I know you have. But I'm afraid you'll have to be a little more patient."

"A little more patient than what? The way our little cowpoke keeps galloping off, he may be a bit 'more patient' than anyone can handle." Andy turned to see Joe pushing his lab cart into the room.

Earlier that morning she'd stopped him as he came out of the elevator and asked if she could talk to him. She'd started to say she was sorry at the same time he was trying to say he was sorry to her. She'd actually started her morning by sharing a laugh with Joe Duffy. Would wonders ever cease? Still, there was no point in being too easy on him. He'd given her some very bad moments. To punish him a little, she didn't laugh out loud at his joke. But it made her smile inside.

"So what is Robbie waiting for?" Joe asked again. He was serious this time.

Andy didn't answer. She shook her head slightly, looked up at the ceiling, and hissed "surprise" quietly between her teeth.

Joe stared at her. "Women," he said and shrugged. "Listen up, Little Buddy," said Joe in a fabulous, fake John Wayne voice. "No need for you-all to go frettin' none. I got me a fantastic surprise, just for you." He pointed right at Robbie.

Don't say "surprise," Andy wanted to yell. But it was too late.

"I don't want no surprises from nobody. They never, ever come anyway," groused Robbie.

Joe looked at the disappointed little boy. "Hey, what did I do? I really do have a surprise for you, Rob." Joe looked at Andy.

She threw up her hands and tried to silence him with a you're-a-nerd look. It went over his head.

"Look, you. When I get my break, you're getting my surprise, whether you like it or not." He tried to chuck Robbie under the chin, but the boy turned his back to him.

Andy took Joe by the hand and pulled him into the hall. "Will you please quit saying 'surprise' to that child? Can't you see how you're upsetting him?"

"I get the feeling there's something going on here, and I don't know what it is. You know, like coming into a movie late and finding the entire audience crying, but you don't see anything so sad."

"Don't be so melodramatic, Joe."

"I'll tell you what my surprise . . . my *treat* for Robbie is, if you'll tell me what's going on. Deal?"

"It's a deal. What's your treat?" In spite of herself, Andy was again beginning to think that Joe Duffy wasn't such a bad guy after all.

"It's not such a big thing, actually. I brought my old gee-tar to work with me today. I thought I might use my hour break to have a sing-along with the kids. I'm no John Denver, and I know it. But I like to sing, and the kids won't care what I sound like."

Andy laughed. "I think that's really nice. I know the kids will love it. I'll bet you don't sound so bad."

"I'm planning this impromptu concert around four. Will you come, Andy?"

"I usually read stories to the children at four. But I could start earlier, say three-thirty. Then you could join us for your surprise. All the children who are ambulatory will be in the play patio. Will that be good for you?"

"Perfect. Do you know you said the forbidden word?"

Andy shook her head.

"Surprise!" he shouted.

Andy jumped. She did it to please him, not because he'd scared her.

"Your turn to explain," he said.

It took only three minutes and a lot of gesturing to describe the surprise project Andy was hoping to get permission for. When she'd told Joe all there was to tell, he was delighted with her idea. He instantly volunteered to join the painting crew. "What a fantastic idea. The kids are going to be wowed," Joe exclaimed, thumping her shoulder in congratulations.

"Ho-oh. Thanks, Joe," she said, wobbling a little. His thump had almost knocked her off her feet. "But I've still got a long way to go before the walls are actually covered with my panoramic dream. I still need the hospital board's permission to paint. Then I need painters to do the painting. Then I need paint for the painters to do the painting with."

Joe laughed. "You're looking at a real artist. I've painted some great-looking walls in my day—with a roller, that is. I bet I could do a fantastic ocean or a very creative sky. I might even be able to work my way up to clouds. I've dreamed of 'painting the clouds with sunshine.' "

"That is so corny," laughed Andy. "You're my very first volunteer. Thanks. Now all I need is a dozen more painters—and the paint."

"Maybe I can help there, too. I just happen to have an Uncle Duffy, who just happens to own a paint store in Culver City. I could take you there. Who knows? We Duffys have always been suckers for a worthy cause—and a pretty face."

Andy felt the blush creep over her cheeks. "Yes. Yes, please, Joe. That would be terrific." She'd beg if she had to. She knew she needed all the help she could possibly get—even Joe Duffy's. Besides, he didn't seem so horrible today. "I'll let you know the minute I get the okay for us to start—if I do."

"Who could resist those imploring Irish green eyes? Well, I guess I'll see you later, around four for the big concert. I'd better get this cart down to the lab now."

"Four. In the play patio. Thank you, Joe."

"For what?"

"For everything. But especially for having an Uncle Duffy with a paint store," answered Andy.

"Lucky break for me, wasn't it? See ya."

Andy watched Joe's retreat until he stepped into the service elevator; then she hurried away in the opposite direction. She didn't want him to turn around and find her staring at him. She didn't know what she wanted. Why was she suddenly so reluctant to take her eyes off him? Only a few days before, she'd never wanted to see him again. You're a puzzle, Andrea Leigh Whitman, she mused. I've never met a girl with more ups and downs than you. How do you feel about Joe Duffy? Just one little clue. "You weird crossword puzzle," she said aloud, and giggled.

"What? Were you speaking to me, Nurse?" asked an elderly gentleman in a white coat. He pushed thick-lensed, wire-framed glasses back up on the bridge of his sharp nose.

"Oh! Dr. Elreden, I'm sorry. I must have been talking to myself," Andy said, embarrassed.

"I understand. Do it myself. Helps me keep my mind orderly. Don't let anyone tell you that talking to yourself means you're the least bit crazy, my dear. You're not crazy until you start answering back." Dr. Elreden chuckled. "So right. So right."

"Thank you, Doctor. I'll remember that." She smiled warmly at him. Dr. Elreden was a favorite of all the nurses and the N.I.T.s. Andy often found him walking along, chatting with himself about a patient who had him worried or an appointment he didn't want to forget. He muttered quite loudly on occasion. And at times he answered himself back, too. He probably hadn't noticed he'd done just that. He was far too busy pushing up his glasses.

During her lunch hour, Andy tucked a couple of books under her arm and walked to the nearby university library. As she crossed the sprawling campus of Bayshore U., she ate her small lunch from a brown bag. Hundreds of people passed. If some of the preoccupied parade made eye contact with her, they smiled. But Bayshore had so many students enrolled in so many different areas of study, and all deeply engrossed in their own worlds and worries, that Andy didn't see one familiar face or exchange one friendly word the entire way.

At the library, as she'd done dozens of times before, she loaded up with stacks of colorful storybooks to read to the children. The section devoted to children's literature was particularly extensive, and she always found something new, plus some old favorites. She'd started making this trip when she'd exhausted the center's meager supply of books. Today she hurried back to the third floor with eight replacements, three of them about Curious George, plus *Peter Pan,* which she had renewed. She spent the rest of the afternoon mulling over the new books and trying to decide which ones she would read that afternoon to her children—and to Joe.

It was almost three-thirty when she gathered up her books from behind the floor desk and went to round up her audience. Her first stop was room four. She was humming a tuneless melody as she entered. "Story time, Heather. Story time, Robbie. Put on your robes and slippers. We have to start earlier today. Wouldn't want to keep Joe waiting," she announced cheerfully.

Heather sat up in her bed; her expression was tense and worried.

Andy was immediately alerted by the girl's behavior. "Where's Robbie, Heather? Is he in the bathroom? Did he already go down to the play patio?"

"I don't know. He went to visit," Heather said softly.

"Whom did he go to visit, honey?"

"Robbie made me promise not to tell."

"Heather, making you promise was wrong for Robbie to do. You have to tell me, honey. You don't want him to miss this wonderful new story about Curious George, do you?" Andy held out the book for Heather to examine."

The child shook her head. "No, I guess not. He said he was going to see Jason," Heather admitted reluctantly.

"Jason? Jason Fox?" asked Andy.

Heather nodded.

That can't be, thought Andy. Robbie knows that Jason has gone home. The alarm bells went off in her head. She did a very quick room search for him. A fast check was all that was necessary to confirm that he'd gone to visit exactly where she'd feared—Jason's house. Once more Robbie Washington was on the loose and probably lost somewhere in the Bayshore Medical Center. She hurried toward the floor desk to give the alarm.

White-clad women in bobbing, starched caps and men in white jackets scurried around the third floor in search of the errant cowboy. Andy couldn't help blaming herself for Robbie's disappearance. She should have kept a closer eye on him. But he hadn't done this since that terrible episode with Dr. Dan and Joe. So why now? The surprise! Of course. Robbie had acted very upset with her and Joe. He'd run off to show her just how angry he was. She'd promised him a surprise, and she hadn't delivered. This had to be Robbie's way of getting even.

"Andy? Andy!" Someone called her. She stopped to wait for Dina Johnson to catch up. "That Robbie. He always picks my shift to pull this. If we don't find him soon . . . well, we have to, that's all."

"You sound seriously worried, Dina. I'm sure he didn't leave the hospital. Robbie's taken off before, and he's never gone far," said Andy, sounding calmer than she actually felt.

"No, that's not what worries me, Andy. The hospital guards would grab him the moment he stepped into the lobby. They've all been notified. It's Robbie's medication. He's overdue now." Dina glanced anxiously up and down the long hall as she spoke.

Andy let her gaze follow Dina's. She wasn't surprised to see Joe, carrying his guitar case, hurrying toward her. But as he reached the door to the nurses' lounge, he pushed it open and went in. At first Andy thought he was just finding a safe place to store his instrument, while he joined in the search. Many minutes later, after Dina sped off to continue her searching, Andy noticed that Joe still hadn't come out of the lounge. She decided to go after him.

"Joe? Joe, I—" Andy was astonished at the scene that greeted her: Joe and Robbie were cuddled together in Mrs. Grymes's oversized green chair, having a private sing-along. Was this where Robbie had been hiding out? She'd never thought to check the lounge, and apparently neither had anyone else.

Joe stopped singing and looked up at Andy. Robbie didn't move. "I hope you don't mind my lending your sweater to my cowboy buddy here?"

"Not at all," said Andy. She raised her eyebrows questioningly and gave Joe a meaningful look. He shook his head. "That's only fair since he let you borrow his hat."

Joe reached up and felt for Robbie's red one-gallon Stetson. With twinkling eyes he pulled it off his head. "I forgot about the hat," he muttered.

"I gave Joe my hat to wear. He's going to let me play his guitar. Huh, Joe?"

"Right, partner."

"I'm afraid that's going to have to wait, now." Andy looked at her watch. "It's almost time for your dinner, Robbie, and your medication. Would you like Joe to carry you back to your room?"

"Can I have a horsey-back ride, Joe?"

"Sure thing, cowboy." Joe stood up and put Robbie down on the couch.

Andy had to stifle her chuckles as she viewed the getup Cowboy Robbie had on. He looked so cute in her old sweater, with his boots sticking out the bottom and his gun bulging on his hip. "Let me help you," she offered.

Joe sat on the couch in front of Robbie, while Andy helped to hoist the small boy up on his wide shoulders. Joe stood up, a bit wobbly at first, then found his footing, and they were off.

Andy followed behind. She made a fast stop at the nurses' station to give the "Robbie's found" report, then quickly ran to catch up to Joe and his rider. She watched the pint-sized cowpoke ride down the hall on Joe's shoulders and remembered the time when a different Joe had complained because Dr. Dan gave Robbie the same horseback ride. Now Robbie was holding on to Joe's hair and happily shouting "Giddyap."

Joe Duffy isn't the same person; he's changed so much, thought Andy. And so have I.

Falling in Like

"COME ON, ROB. You've got to sit still, or I won't be able to carry you," said Joe.

Andy noticed Robbie's sudden change from the cowboy, loping along on his favorite old horse, to rodeo rider, jerking and swaying on a bucking bronco. She was just about to warn Joe to be careful with his passenger when she realized it wasn't Joe who was doing the erratic bouncing. "Joe! Robbie's having a seizure," shouted Andy.

Together they eased Robbie down from his precarious perch. Quickly they carried him into his room.

"Joe, on the floor. Here."

"How can I help, Andy?" asked Joe, when Robbie was stretched out on the tile between them.

"Hand me a pillow from the bed; then ring the emergency button."

Joe wasted no time getting to the button and pressing it for help, but he never took his eyes off Andy and Robbie. "Where are they?" asked Joe impatiently, as Andy began the familiar procedure to ensure Robbie's safety during a convulsion. "Everyone must be asleep," hissed Joe. His agitation was increasing.

"You go for help, Joe. I can manage here. The whole pediatric floor is always in confusion at dinner time. With half the staff hunting for Robbie, they've probably fallen behind. Try the play patio. That's where the children should be. Someone may already be bringing them back to their rooms.''

"You just hang in there, sweetheart. I'll be back with someone." He pushed the emergency button again, then raced down the hall.

Robbie's seizure was brief and, for him, fairly mild. His condition began to improve rapidly. His medication must be getting close to regulation and starting to work for him, thought Andy happily, as she gently lifted the now calm child onto his bed.

In moments, Joe returned with Dr. Dan and one of the floor nurses. Andy quickly explained what had happened, while the doctor examined Robbie. With a pleased smile, he announced that Robbie would be fine; the crisis had passed.

Dr. Dan patted her shoulder. "Andréa is one of the finest nurses we have in pediatrics," he said to the nurse with him. The nurse smiled and nodded her head. "We both think so, don't we, Mrs. Grymes?"

Andy hadn't noticed her supervisor enter the room. Now she turned to find her standing next to Joe. Just once, Andy thought to herself, let her say yes without any qualifications.

"Yes, Doctor. *One* of our best," agreed Mrs. Grymes.

Andy raised her eyebrows and smiled at Joe, who stood slightly behind the supervisor. He winked at her.

"Well, now, Andrea, Joe," Mrs. Grymes said. "Everything here seems to be in competent hands, doesn't it? I suggest you two take a short break to catch your breath before returning to the floor. Shall we say ten minutes?" Getting no answer, she went on. "Why don't you go sit down in the nurses' lounge? Have a cup of tea and relax.''

"I should be getting back to the lab, Mrs. Grymes. They're probably wondering what's happened to me," said Joe.

"I'll take care of the lab. You two go along." Mrs. Grymes turned on her heel and moved quickly to the in-hospital phone at the floor desk.

As they passed, she was talking in hushed tones to someone in the lab department. They heard her wheeling the ten-minute break out of Joe's supervisor. She sounded exceptionally gracious and charming. Andy shot Joe a who-is-that-lovely-person-in-Mrs.-Grymes's-body look. He laughed and shrugged.

"I guess our Simon LeGrymes isn't such an old witch after all. Under that grim exterior beats a heart of—"

Andy interrupted Joe. "Don't get carried away. A kind word doesn't mean she's Glinda, the Good Witch of the North, you know."

He shrugged again, then held the lounge door open for Andy before following her in.

"How do you like your . . . ?" Andy was walking to the table that held the coffee machine and the hot plate with water for tea. She stopped and looked at Joe.

"Coffee, thanks," he finished for her. "Cream, no sugar."

Andy carried his coffee and her tea over to the small couch where Joe was sitting. She handed him his cup and sat down in the big green chair facing him. They shared the footstool between them. "Umm. Good," she sighed, sipping from her steaming mug.

"Does nursing ever get to you, Andy? These poor kids seem to have so much pain and disappointment to bear. Don't you ever feel like going home and staying there?" Joe stared into his cup as he spoke. His sky blue eyes were hooded by half-closed lids. Still, Andy could see that some of their usual twinkle had faded. The corners of his mouth seemed to sag from the weight of his thoughts.

"Of course I do. But there are a lot of positive things in nursing, too. Our kids at Bayshore get loving care, not just routine medical attention. There's a wonderful feeling of hope here, Joe. And peace of mind."

"And there's death here. Sometimes there's death." Joe put his cup on the floor and dropped his head into his hands.

Without thinking, Andy put her tea on the table next to the couch and went to sit beside him. She reached out and gently stroked the soft curls at the back of his neck. "What is it, Joe? Is something wrong?" she asked softly.

"It's Donny Masters. I really liked that kid."

Andy sighed. "We all did. He was a sweet child."

"They're all sweet kids. And they all deserve to live full, happy lives. And they don't all get to. They should grow up, Andy. That's what kids are supposed to do." When he looked at her, she saw so much despair in his eyes that it tore at her heart. With the lightest touch, she pushed a stray lock of jet black hair from his forehead.

"Of course you're right. But that isn't something we decide," she told him.

"Donny was doing so great. He'd been in remission for almost five years. I swear to you, Andy, that everybody in oncology and the lab thought he had a chance to beat it. I mean, we were all so hopeful."

"I know, Joe."

"Even as an outpatient, he always came to see me. If I wasn't in the lab, he'd sneak up here to pedi-3 to find me. Do you know that I took the blood sample that brought him back into the hospital? He was in so much pain, and I was the only one he'd let touch him."

"You're blaming yourself for finding Donny's cancer, Joe. That's wrong. The cancer was there, and it was killing him. Your job was to find that out, in the quickest possible way, so that the doctors could help him."

"But they didn't help him. All my life I've wanted to be a pediatrician. I've never even considered any other branch of medicine. But what good is it, if one of the best little kids in the world dies? Why bother?"

"Because the very same doctors who couldn't keep Donny Masters from dying gave him five good years to live. And they gave Jason Fox the opportunity to be like other little boys, with two legs to walk on. They made him whole again; they gave him hope. And what about Robbie? His seizure this evening was the mildest one yet. When he entered Bayshore, his epilepsy was out of control. Now he's almost there—almost on the road to being seizure-free." She had nothing more to say, but her words hadn't been just for him. Andy knew she, too, needed reassuring. There was a reason she kept coming back—the children.

The anger and tension in Joe's face seemed to melt away, and the corners of his lips lifted into a grateful smile. He unclenched his hands, rubbing the circulation back into them, then slipped them around Andy's waist. They rested there softly. There was something about his holding her that she liked. She even found her own hands lying gently on on his shoulders.

"When I'm a pediatrician, I want you to be my nurse," said Joe. "You're everything a nurse should be. In fact, you're everything a woman should be." He took her hand and held it for a moment, staring at it intently; then he got up from the couch and led her to the lounge door.

Andy was about to step into the hall, when Joe's grasp pulled her back to him. She looked up into his thickly lashed blue eyes and waited.

"Andy?"

"Yes, Joe."

"Would you . . . ? Do you think you'd like to . . . ?"

"Yes, Joe?"

"Go to the movies with me on Saturday? At night? If I'm off, that is?"

"Yes, Joe. I'd love to."

"You would? You will? Great. Okay. I'll pick you up at seven. Is that all right?"

"Seven's fine. You know where I live." It wasn't a question— and she knew Joe knew it was meant as a friendly poke in the ribs.

Rated R

ANDY FELT STRANGE inside—nervous, excited, and scared. It surprised her that being with Joe could make her feel that way. When he'd arrived to pick her up, she'd felt fine. Everything was exactly as it should be—a perfectly normal event, like any boy, anywhere, picking up his date. He smiled, shook her dad's hand, and helped her on with her new white satin baseball jacket. He'd held the door for her and promised Big Andy he'd bring her home at a reasonable hour. He'd walked beside her to the passenger side of Daisy, his beloved old Chevy, and yanked open the door, closing it with a slam after she got in. What was strange about any of that? Andy couldn't think of one strange thing so far—unless you counted the fact that they hadn't spoken a single word to one another yet. She decided to be brave. She'd speak first.

"You look nice in that sweater."

"I like your jacket," Joe said at the exact same time.

Andy smiled uncomfortably and clamped her lips tightly together. This was like her very first date with a boy all over again. She gave a nervous giggle, then was silent. She stared at her hands. He stared at the road.

When she casually tried to sneak a peek at his profile, she found he was sneaking a peek at her. They both laughed with an embarrassed titter. Now Andy felt even worse than strange; she felt utterly foolish. For a brief moment, she contemplated jumping out and escaping at the next signal. Where's your gumption? Your natural spunk? she asked herself. She decided to give it one more try.

"I—"

"So—" Joe cut her off again. Another deafening silence followed. "You first, okay?" he finally said.

Andy nodded. "I was just going to say how much better your car looks since the last time I saw it."

"Yup. That was the night I had to rescue you from the clutches of Bayshore Medical's greatest intern and lover. I've been working on Daisy a lot since then."

Why did he have to bring up Collin? Andy fumed silently. I'd almost forgotten that whole loathsome experience. She faced the side window and feigned interest in the other cars on the street. She no longer wanted to talk.

"What I said. . . . That was dumb, wasn't it? I'm sorry," he apologized. "You didn't want to be reminded of that night."

She turned to face him again.

"I have this etiquette book on good dating manners. My big brother, John, gave it to me. It says, 'When the conversation starts to lag, be sure to mention any experiences you've shared or may have in common with your date.' The book was John's before he gave it to me. I swear it. Now that I think about it, that's probably why he's still not married—and why he gave me the book. I think I picked the wrong shared experience to mention, huh?"

Andy couldn't stop her tiny giggles. "Uh-huh. But that's all right. Let's forget all about it; I'd rather."

"Me too," Joe agreed with a flashing smile. "What movie would you like to see—for a better shared experience?"

"You choose. Anything will be a treat. I almost never find time to go to a movie. You name it; I've never seen it."

"There's a great-adventure-swashbuckling-romantic-comedy-with-definite-dramatic-appeal movie playing in Westwood Village."

"That sounds great. What's it called?" asked Andy.

"The Great-Adventure-Swashbuckling-Romantic-Comedy-with-Definite-Dramatic-Appeal Movie! What do you say?"

"I'd love it. That's exactly the kind of picture I wanted to see. Dare I ask who's starring in it?"

"The Muppets!"

"Oh, Joe, I love the Muppets. I watch them on TV whenever I can. I was so disappointed when they canceled the series. Weren't you? Don't you love Miss Piggy?"

"*Moi?* But of course. I relate to Kermie better, though."

"Because you're both green?" teased Andy.

"Well, that, and because we're both handsome Irish lads, don't you know," said Joe in a thick brogue.

"That sounds fantastic. Say something else. I love a brogue."

"Then you'd be lovin' the Duffy household," said Joe.

For the rest of the ride into Westwood, there were no more uncomfortable silences. The air was sparked with enough Irish brogue to fill Daisy with shamrocks.

They walked side by side from the public parking lot to the theater about three blocks away. Andy couldn't help noticing how much it cost to park Daisy in the lot. This was going to be an expensive evening for Joe. Remembering the condition of his old car, she wondered if he could really afford it.

"I don't believe it. Would you look at that line? We're over half an hour early—and a day late," grumbled Joe.

"It looks as if it wraps around the block twice," agreed Andy. "Even if we wait, we probably won't get in until the second showing."

"And if we go get something to eat or walk around Westwood for an hour, we'll be so far back that we'll miss the second show, too. But I promised you Miss Piggy, and Miss Piggy you get," said Joe.

"That's silly. I don't have to go to this particular movie. I'll bet there are bunches of them in Westwood I haven't seen—all with shorter lines, too. Why don't we walk around and take a look?"

"Okay. Sure. Why not?" A look of relief swept over Joe's face. He took Andy's hand tightly in his own and led her through the crowd of Muppet fans to the corner. "Which way? Right or left?" he asked.

"Right. I'm positive that's the way to go." She felt she'd also been right about not asking Joe to stand in line. Two rights in one night. Where Joe Duffy was concerned, that was a first. "A worthy record," she thought aloud.

"What is?"

"What is what?"

"A worthy record."

"Oh. The . . . um . . . number of people who are willing to stand in line for hours to see a Muppet movie. I think that says a lot for the Muppets and the little child in all of us. Did you notice that the crowd was mostly adults?" She was talking fast to change the subject and had to gasp for air at the end of her sentence.

"Do you want to go back for Miss Piggy? Really, I don't mind. We can wait in line if you'd like."

"No. That's not what I meant." Out of the frying pan, as they say, she scolded herself.

"It's just that I wanted to take you someplace special after the movie. I didn't want to waste time standing in a line. We don't have all night. I promised to get you home at a reasonable hour, remember?"

"Where are we going afterward? Which someplace special?"

"Someplace special to me. I hope you'll think so, too." They crossed the street. "But it's a surprise. So forget it for now and find us a show. How about that one?" Joe pointed at the marquee glowing above them.

"Are you sure? It's a love story. And it's rated R."

"You mean to tell me you're not old enough to go into an R-rated picture? I've robbed the pediatric ward's cradle?"

"Don't worry. I'm old enough for an R-rated picture. It's just that I've heard something about this movie from my friends and. . . ."

"And . . . ?"

"And it's very . . . I mean—"

"Sexy?"

"Well, yes. I guess you could call it that."

"There's no one I'd rather see a sexy movie with than you, Andy. Besides, the line's short."

Reluctantly she allowed him to drag her to the end of the line. Going to an R-rated movie with a boy she hardly knew could cause problems, she warned herself. He might get ideas—the wrong ideas—as Collin Ellis had. But when you stop to think about it, she decided, Collin got his wrong ideas at a very unsexy skating rink, not an R-rated movie. I guess, for the idea to be wrong, the boy has to be wrong. She wondered if Joe could be the right boy for her? Three "Joe Duffy rights" in one night! That would be too much to hope for. If he wasn't her Mr. Right, it wasn't because he wasn't trying.

Andy felt her heart beat in double time as his fingers played over her hand. With each circle his thumb made on the back of her wrist, the tiny hairs at the curve of her neck stood up, as if she'd been given an electrical shock. Mr. Right or Mr. Wrong, she had to admit Joe's touch was playing havoc with her pulse. She hoped a phlebotomist couldn't automatically tell when a person was suffering from a rapid heartbeat—like hers.

"Andy! Joe! Are we glad we found you."

Both Andy and Joe turned to see who was calling to them.

Andy waved enthusiastically at Jackee, Monica, and Peter, Monica's thirteen-year-old brother, who'd been visiting from San Francisco for a few days. "Hey. Hi, you guys," she called back. They all came over to join Andy and Joe.

"Hello, ladies," Joe said gallantly. "Who's the short person, Monica?" He stood eye to eye with Peter.

"My brother, Peter Ross, this is Joe Duffy. Joe works at Bayshore in the lab while he's studying to be a doctor. And Joe, Petey's just a growing boy of thirteen going on fourteen."

"And six feet going on seven," added Jackee.

Peter gave her a dirty look.

Joe shook Peter's hand. "Thirteen, huh? He makes you look as if you're standing in a hole, Monica," he joked.

Peter sighed.

"My whole family is like that, except my mom. Out of three children, I'm the only one under six feet tall," Monica explained.

"No cuts, buddy," said a surly voice from the line behind Joe.

"They're not cutting in," said Andy. Her nerves were on edge already; the last thing she needed was another *experience* where Joe had to rescue her.

"Of course they aren't. They're friends. *Okay?*" asked Joe. His look dared the unpleasant man to ask their friends to leave.

"Cool, kid. No sweat. Be my guest," the man offered in a much nicer tone of voice.

Andy was instantly relieved to know that Jackee and Monica would be seeing the movie with Joe and her. With them right beside her, what could possibly happen?

"You were wonderful, Joe," sang Jackee, slinging an arm around his waist and hugging. "We would've waited in line forever. I wonder where all these people came from? The line's suddenly a hundred miles long."

"I bet they're all from Muppetsville, don't you, Andy?" Joe squeezed Jackee back.

Andy nodded and smiled. She wished she could be like Jackee. She wished she had the nerve to hug Joe if she felt like hugging him. Her thoughts made flashes of embarrassment flood her cheeks. Why had she thought that? She didn't want to hug Joe—did she?

"Andy, you're blushing," whispered Monica. "If having us cut into line embarrasses you, we can go to the end. It doesn't matter," she offered.

"No, Monica. I don't want you to go. Please?" Andy's eyes pleaded with her friend to stay with her.

"Then I'll bet you're blushing because we caught you and Joe holding hands, right?" Monica whispered and smiled knowingly.

Andy choked. "No. No," she protested in a hoarse gurgle.

The line began to move, and she was saved from having to say anything more. They looked like any ordinary group of five friends going to the movies together. They laughed and chatted among themselves as they walked in single file down the theater aisle to search for five seats together. Then, one by one, they crawled over the legs of the people already seated.

Joe went first, saying "Excuse me" over and over. Then came Andy with "I'm sorry; excuse me; I'm sorry" until she reached the seat next to Joe and sat down. After Andy came Jackee, Monica, and Peter. They shifted and twisted in their seats until they found the most comfortable position for film watching, whispered together, and waited for the theater to grow dim, signaling the start of the picture.

Andy felt as if she were sitting on hot coals. Every muscle in her body seemed to be twitching madly. She willed herself to sit still. To everyone else in the theater, they appeared to be five friends on a movie outing. To Andy, there was no one else in their row besides herself and Joe. When he took her hand in the darkness, she felt the twitching grow worse.

She blocked from her mind the feeling of Joe's strong fingers entwined with hers. That worked for almost three minutes. She refused to feel the gentle touch of his thumb, once more caressing—this time the palm of her hand. Her refusal went unheeded; she couldn't feel anything but his tingling touch.

Concentrate on something else, she told herself. She stared intently at the flashing screen before her. That was the worst thing she could have done. The brightly glowing, flickering images that danced before her eyes made her breath catch in her throat. The most beautiful music in the world seemed to be playing for the swaying figures, who rhythmically melted together as they danced across the screen. When the man in the film stopped dancing to stare into his partner's eyes, Andy felt as if he looked into her eyes, too—and could see her soul. Her heart thundered, and she looked away, only to meet Joe's eyes staring at her in the same pulse-quickening way. She forced herself to look back at the screen.

The entire theater was filled with the sight and the sounds of the passion the two screen lovers created before her. When their lips met in a deep, meaningful kiss, Andy felt an unbearable excitement race through her body. She couldn't look away. Each embrace they shared made her want to move closer to the boy who sent the same shivers of excitement up her arm. And each embrace they shared

129

made her want to run out of the darkened theater and into the fresh, sobering night air, away from him.

But she knew she'd sit there. She couldn't climb over her friends, who would ask in concerned voices what the matter was. And she knew she couldn't bear to have Joe stop holding her hand.

"This movie is disgusting," blared Peter during one of the most romantic scenes of the film. "They actually had the guts to charge us five bucks to see this goosh?"

Shushes came from several different areas of the theater.

"Peter, please," pleaded Monica. "They'll throw us out."

"Good. I don't want to spend my last night in L.A. being tortured. If I did, I could have stayed in San Francisco and let Mom nag me to death."

"Peter, if your sister doesn't sock you, I'm going to," warned Jackee.

"I'm hungry," Peter retorted.

"Look. Why don't I get us all some popcorn? Just enough to tide us over till the end of the movie," offered Joe.

"Yeah," agreed Peter happily.

"You don't have to do that," said Monica.

Andy wanted to poke her.

"Yes, he does, Sis. Leave him alone. Please go, Joe," begged Peter woefully.

Andy could have kissed Peter.

Joe got up and maneuvered his way as quickly as possible past the row of agitated movie-watchers.

With him gone, Andy took her first really deep breath for nearly an hour, but her hands were still shaking.

"What's going on between you two?" whispered Jackee, when Joe was out of hearing range.

"Nothing is going on," Andy whispered back.

"I didn't know that 'nothing' required a guy to rub the skin off a girl's hand. Yours must be rubbed nearly raw," snickered Jackee.

Monica was listening. She leaned across Jackee to join the buzzing exchange. "I certainly wish I could get a little 'nothing' going in my life, Andy." She cleared her throat knowingly.

130

"Ssh, you two. I'm trying to watch the picture," hissed Andy.

"All right! Thanks, Joe," came Peter's genuine but loud appreciation, as Joe handed him a box of popcorn. "Buttered! This is great. Just the way I like it."

Joe patted him on the head and delivered a box to Monica and Jackee to share. The last box he handed to Andy, then sat down.

The one and only time that Andy put her hand in the popcorn box, she encountered Joe's hand reaching in, too. The few kernels she picked up, before abruptly withdrawing her hand, were quickly popped into her mouth. She almost choked on them, her mouth was so dry. She left the rest of the popcorn eating to Joe, who didn't seem to notice that he finished off the whole box himself.

When "The End" finally appeared on the screen, Andy tried to spring out of her seat. Joe still held her hand and, with his shoulder pressed against her, she couldn't stand.

At last the house lights came up, and the audience rose to begin the mass exodus from the theater. Gratefully Andy followed the crowd. Nervous with anticipation, she once more stood under the glaring illumination of the theater's old-fashioned marquee. She was all smiles, as she chatted and joked with her friends and tried to appear much calmer outside than she felt inside.

They were saying good night. She tried desperately to prolong that moment. What would happen when she was finally alone with Joe? Monica and Jackee wouldn't be there to protect her—from herself! She told herself that she was being ridiculous. It was, after all, only simple, everyday, hand-holding. She held people's hands a thousand times every day. It had never kept her from making intelligent conversation before. Why should it keep her from talking to Joe? She knew she'd die if she had to live through one more of those lengthy silences.

"I'm glad I finally had a chance to get to know you both," said Joe. "I want to know all of Andy's friends."

"You're our friend, too, now," said Monica. "After all, you did feed us popcorn."

"And I'm still starving. When do we eat?" groaned Peter.

"You're always hungry, Petey," said Monica. "We'll be going in a minute. You can hang on."

"Well, it's been great talking to you, Joe. If all the Duffys are as nice as you are, how about finding two more just like you for Monica and me?" suggested Jackee, with a gleeful grin.

"I'll do my best," offered Joe.

"You'd better take good care of Joe, Andy. I think Jackee is planning to bet you double or nothing for him," Monica teased.

"Food. Food. I need food," moaned the staggering Peter.

"We'd better go," said Jackee, eyeing Peter's antics and shaking her head.

Good-byes were exchanged one last time. Andy stood next to Joe and watched her friends walk away. The butterflies in her stomach felt like pterodactyls.

"Your friends are great." Joe took her hand and caused the pterodactyls to rampage.

She smiled weakly and nodded. She was sure that Jackee had been humming something she wanted Andy to hear, as she walked away. The tune sounded familiar, but she just couldn't remember what it was.

They were in the car, and Joe had started Daisy's engine when Andy remembered the name of Jackee's song. It was a very old song—the kind they called a standard: "All or Nothing at All." Andy didn't want to bet double or nothing with Jackee, but did she want him all?

"Now for my special place," announced Joe.

14

Duffys by the Dozen

JOE CHANGED LANES and parallel-parked the car in front of an old-style English pub, right out of the Elizabethan Age. Its swinging wooden sign announced to the world that this was, indeed, Duff's Tavern! She burst out laughing.

"What's so funny?" asked Joe. He seemed surprised by her laughter.

"I don't believe it, that's all. There really is a special place for Joe Duffy to go—a Duff's Tavern."

"It is special to the Duffys, but it's extra special to me. You're the first girl I've ever brought here to meet—it." He smiled quizzically.

Andy's stomach did giant flip-flops. She was the first. "Well, lead on, MacDuff. I can hardly wait to see this wonderful secret of yours," she said enthusiastically.

"You're the secret," he whispered, opening the door to the pub and ushering her in with a slight bow. "Duff's has been waiting to meet you for a long, long time."

Now Andy felt confused. "I thought I was coming to see your favorite place. Why would a pub want to meet me?"

"Duff's is my favorite place, full of my favorite people. I want you to meet them. I've told them so much about my favorite girl, they're pretty excited about meeting you, too."

133

His favorite girl. She was feeling wonderful, terrific, better than that, as Joe took her hand in his.

"This is lovely." Andy admired the mahogany paneling and the long bar to the left with its gleaming brass and mirrors. Booths with brass-studded seats lined the wall on the right; and neat, oak tables were scattered in the space between booths and bar. Centered on each table was a bud vase containing fern and a green-tipped white carnation. The brass fixtures shed enough light so that patrons could see, but were dim enough to keep the pub cozy. "Enchanting old English," she said, over the clink of silver and the mumble of conversation. Tempting aromas floated in the air.

"I think Duff would rather you called it enchanted old Irish." Joe laughed. "He swears this place is frequented by the little people. He only lets big people who truly believe in leprechauns come here."

"If I didn't believe before, I do now," gasped Andy, as she watched the round-faced man with curly red hair bounce toward them. He looked like one of the magical little people. His rosy cheeks glowed with high spirits. His eyes glittered mischievously. Andy liked him even before she met him.

"Well, now, if it isn't Joe Duffy himself." He beamed at Joe, reaching up to pat his head and muss his shining black curly hair. "So you finally brought her." Now Andy shared the warmth of his smile with Joe. "You must be Joe's Andy." He put out his hand.

Nodding her agreement, Andy slipped her hand into his. It disappeared into his warm grasp. "Yes, I guess I am," she mumbled.

"Well, I'm Duff," he said, shaking her hand with such exuberance that her head bobbed. "Mother, you'd better be gettin' out here and see what Joe's brought us," he called over his shoulder. "She's a darlin', she is."

The double doors, which Andy guessed led to the kitchen, flew open and a tiny woman with a glorious mane of silver and black hair burst into the room. Andy sensed she'd been waiting anxiously behind them for just such a summons. She rushed over to Joe and planted a kiss on the cheek he had to lower for her.

"Andy," Joe said, "I'd like you to meet my mom, Kathleen Duffy. And my pop, Kevin Duffy."

Joe's father was still pumping her hand with such vigor that his mother could only exchange smiles with her.

All the Duffys smile with their eyes, thought Andy. But Kathleen's were an extraordinary sky blue, exactly like the heavily lashed eyes of her son. Joe's eyes *are* beautiful, she suddenly realized. Why hadn't she noticed before?

"Hello, darlin'. You call me Kate. I'm either Mom or Kate to everyone who knows me, except Duff here." She smiled at Andy in a way that said more than words about her feelings for Joe's father. "And this great lummox who's workin' so hard at pullin' your arm off, you can call him Duff."

"And I guess you know who I am," Joe teased his mother.

"And how should I? With you spendin' all your time in the hospital or at the university?" A rippling laugh followed Kate's pretend anger, and she tweaked her son's ear. "I hope you two are hungry. I've got something special for you just simmerin' away in the kitchen. Duff, where're your manners, love? What kind of host are you? Find the children a nice table."

"The best one in the house—when we're full up, like tonight."

"The best table in the house, Andy, is the one that's empty when a customer comes in. Don't let Pop's Irish tongue fool you," warned Joe.

"Impossible. I've had plenty of practice with his son," Andy shot back.

"She's a feisty one, son, but that's how I like them," laughed Duff. He winked at his wife, and she swished a get-away-with you hand at him, then turned toward the kitchen, while Duff led Joe and Andy to a table near the back.

"Don't encourage Andy, Pop. You wouldn't believe how prickly Nurse Whitman can get," Joe said, as she slid into the chair his father held for her.

This time his teasing didn't make her angry. She was feeling too good. She was too happy. She laughed along with Joe and his father.

"Now, Whitman, is it? Seems to me, I've known a Whitman or two." Duff wrinkled his forehead and rubbed his chin.

"That's exactly what Big Andy said when I first mentioned Joe: that he knew a lot of Duffys," said Andy.

"Now Big Andy Whitman! Of course." He put a hand on her shoulder. "You must be the lieutenant's little girl. Fine man, your father," said Duff.

"You know my dad?" asked Andy.

"I've had the pleasure. My nephew, Brian Duffy, works with your father out of Detectives at the Venice Division. Joe, do you remember the night we threw that bash for Brian, when he was assigned to Metro? The lieutenant came to Brian's party. It was right here at Duff's Tavern. And a fine party it was."

Andy cocked her head and turned to stare at Joe. He nodded his head sheepishly.

"You mean you already knew my dad before—"

"I wasn't really positive I knew him until that night I brought you your books. When you didn't seem too thrilled to see me, your dad and I thought it would be better if you got to know me before I told you he and I knew each other. You might have felt we were setting you up. You're not angry, are you?" he asked.

"How could she be? There's no woman alive can resist the Duffy charm. Right, Andy?" asked his father.

"Right. Joe's charming. Just charming," she said with a sarcasm that made all three laugh.

"Well, here it is. And a better pea soup you'll never eat," promised Kate, swinging through the kitchen doors, this time with a heavily laden tray in her hands.

"Let me take that, Mom." Joe jumped to his feet and relieved his mother of her burden.

"You'd have made a talented restaurateur," said Duff. "A man fit to follow in his father's footsteps."

"What he'll be makin' is a talented doctor, Kevin Duffy. And followin' in nobody's footsteps. Joe will be makin' footsteps of his own," corrected Kate.

"And let me guess who he's thinking about making his own special nurse," said a lilting voice behind Andy.

She turned her head to see who'd spoken. She knew she was staring, but she couldn't help it. Standing behind her were three full-color reproductions of Kevin Duffy—one in the giant economy size.

"Andy," said Joe, "I'm sorry to say this big redheaded character is John MacDougal Duffy, my older brother—the one who gave me the etiquette book, remember?" Joe raised his eyebrows and rolled his eyes heavenward.

Shared experiences, she remembered. Andy nodded. She stood up and put out her hand to shake John's. He'd inherited more than red hair and twinkling green eyes from his father. John, too, pumped her hand vigorously.

"And those two Irish beauties sizing you up so slyly from behind John's back are my twin sisters, Colleen and Corrine," Joe continued.

"At least he didn't call us his *older* sisters. That's something to be grateful for. I'm Colleen," said one of the girls.

"And I'm Corrine. Glad you came. Joe's said so many lovely things about you; we've all been eager to meet you."

Although she was sure she'd never met any of the Duffys before, the twins looked very familiar. Andy tried to remember where she might have seen them, but nowhere came to mind. "I'm glad Joe brought me to meet you, too. I think Duff's Tavern is quite a grand place," said Andy. She looked at Joe. The Duffy brogue was catching.

" 'A grand place,' she said. Did you hear that, Mother? Our lad's found himself a clever girl," said Duff.

Kate looked at Duff and smiled conspiratorially.

Andy felt her cheeks flame.

"Enough talkin'. Can't you see you're embarrassing the poor child? And my soup's gettin' cold. Sit down, darlin'; eat something. There's a loaf of fresh-baked bread and plenty of butter to go along with the broth. Joe, you serve Andy. Duff, get yourself in the kitchen; I've somethin' to say to you."

Duff winked at Joe and Andy, but he followed Kate docilely.

"It's been quite *grand* meeting you, Andy. I can see you're truly going to get along with the Duffy clan. Just enough of the old blarney to fit right in," John joked, stressing the "grand" to tease Andy. All the Duffys seemed to be teases, too.

The twins nodded, agreeing with John.

Andy smiled and thanked him for the compliment—she guessed.

All four of them laughed.

"I'd better get back to my bartending before the customers, surly lot that they are, begin breaking things to get my attention. It really has been nice meeting you." John pumped her hand again.

"Us, too," said Colleen. "I don't usually work here, unless Pop knows he's in for a big night, like tonight; then I fill in. So far this evening I've played the hostess with the mostest; Flo, the waitress; and a busperson the Marx Brothers would have been proud of. I dumped a whole tray of dirty dishes in the middle of the kitchen floor."

"And I slipped on the mess she dropped," added Corrine in a disgusted voice. "During the daylight hours, Colleen's an actress and a model. Thank heavens she only moonlights at Duff's. We could never afford to have her fill in full-time," she teased.

"Model, yes—actress, I'm beginning to wonder about. . . ."

The rest of Colleen's words became a blur to Andy. That's where I've seen them—or at least Colleen, she thought. She's the gorgeous redhead Joe was having dinner with the night I went out with Jackee and Monica to the Little Small Café. The sudden rush of unexpected relief that flooded through Andy's body at this realization surprised her. She was beginning to care about Joe, and she was very glad the Duffy family seemed to like her.

"Come on, Colleen. There are are plenty of dishes for you to break, all still sitting on customers' tables. We'd better get to work before Pop comes to get us," said pretty Corrine. "See you two later." She leaned over and gave Joe a peck on the cheek. There was a bright smile for Andy.

"She's right. Mom's the head cook, but Corrine's not too shabby herself. If she stays away too long, Mom will try to do it all. But I'm really useless. Frankly, no one would miss my helpful hands," confessed Colleen with a tiny laugh. "But I'd still better get back, too."

Her red-lipped smile was so brilliant it dazzled. She turned and headed for the kitchen behind her sister.

"Soup's on," said Joe, taking the lid off the steaming tureen Kate had brought them. He ladled out the enticingly aromatic soup.

"Umm," murmured Andy after her first taste. "Umm. . . . Umm," she uttered after each mouthful.

"Did anyone ever tell you that you have a tendency to repeat yourself?" asked Joe. He, too, was downing the soup as quickly as he could after blowing each spoonful cool.

"Oh, this is wonderful." Andy hungrily consumed her soup. She was thoroughly enjoying the rich Garlic broth, filled with chunks of ham, carrots, potatoes, and small bits of peas. It was thick enough to eat with a fork, but she intended to use her spoon. She didn't want to miss a single drop.

"Have a slice of Mom's potato bread while I fill your bowl again." Joe handed her one of the extra thick slices he'd lavishly slathered with butter.

Andy passed Joe her empty bowl. "I'm sorry. I must look like Miss Piggy. But your mother makes the best split-pea soup I've ever eaten. I didn't know I was this hungry until I took that first sip. Then. . . ."

"Mom's going to love you for that." He gave her the refilled bowl.

While she waited for it to cool, Andy popped a piece of Kate's freshly baked bread into her mouth. "Everything your mom makes is delicious."

"Mmmhmm," Joe answered, his mouth full of soup.

Andy finished her second bowl much more slowly and, she hoped, in quieter slurps. Two bowls of soup were gone. Two buttery slices of bread were gone. She wiped her mouth with a napkin and reluctantly pushed her empty bowl away. "I'd burst if I ate another drop," she sighed.

"Me, too."

"Joe! Joe! Joe!" Suddenly they were besieged by three teenagers. Andy didn't have to be told that they were Duffys, too. She may

139

not have known which was which, but she was getting to know an authentic Duffy when she saw one.

"Okay. Okay, you hooligans. I'm glad to see you, too." He hugged and kissed each of the girls and exchanged pats on the back with the boy. "You'd think I lived in Antarctica and worked at a polar bear hospital the way you three are acting."

"But we never get to see you anymore," said the lovely girl with Kevin Duffy's fiery red hair.

"Matty's right," said a slightly older, but equally attractive girl with the same coloring as Joe.

"You mad at me too, Jamey?" asked Joe.

Andy was sure that Jamey looked exactly as Joe must have looked when he was fourteen or fifteen. He was a very good-looking young man.

"Naw. A fellow's got a lot of things to take care of. I know you were busy, Joe, or you'd have come home," said the boy.

"Come home?" asked Andy.

"I never mentioned it, but I have a small place near the university—kind of like a guest cottage. It's really rent-free, but I pay my own utilities and the phone bill. I also have to do some general gardening and fix-it stuff for the owner. The house is on his estate."

"It sounds nice," said Andy.

"It's terrible," said the youngest girl. "He's so busy at the hospital and with school, he never even comes home to eat with us anymore. You used to, Joe. Now when you have free time, you go out." She shot Andy an unpleasant look.

"By the way, this is Andy. *The* Andy, Matty," Joe said. "And this sweet child with such a sour face is Matty. She's my second-youngest sister. She's sixteen, but not always sweet."

Matty made a face at him.

"And this is Megan. She's eighteen."

Megan's smile was just like Joe's.

"And this very handsome guy is Jamey. He's fourteen. And then there's Molly. She's the youngest."

"Molly's only twelve," Jamey informed Andy. "And she's spending the night at her friend Hillary's house."

140

"What are you three doing here so late? Don't teenagers sleep anymore?" Joe asked.

"We went to the movies with Rosalee and her dad, Mr. Levine," explained Megan.

With her wild mane of black curls, her rosy cheeks, and her pert smile, Megan could never be mistaken for anyone but Kate's daughter. But unlike Kate, Joe, and Jamey, Megan had lovely green eyes, the color of spring leaves. Andy marveled at the entire Duffy family. Each member was so attractive in his or her own way. Only good-looking people got to be Duffys, she decided. And Joe had to be the best-looking Duffy of all.

"We have to go, Meg. I promised Andy's dad I'd get her home before midnight," said Joe.

"If not, I'll turn into a pumpkin," joked Andy. But right now, I feel like Cinderella at the ball, she thought silently.

"The pub's emptying. I was going to see if Mom wanted to leave early with me and the brats, anyway. John can drop Pop off on his way home. Well, I hope I'll see you again, Andy," Megan said.

"Me too, Megan. I'm glad we met. I'm glad I met all the Duffys," Andy said sincerely.

"Even me?" asked Joe.

"Especially you," answered Andy before she could stop the words from coming out. The heat from her blushing cheeks could have made soup simmer. My blushing is becoming a habit, she thought. Whenever I'm with Joe, words seem to come out of my mouth that I can't believe I've said.

She was glad that Joe kept their good-byes short. Andy did make a special trip into the kitchen to compliment Kate on her delicious soup and wonderful bread. Kate hugged her, and they spent five minutes thanking each other. The twins were up to their elbows in soapy water, waving sudsy hands at her, when she called her good-byes. A wave to John, cleaning up behind the bar, and a kiss on the cheek from Duff at the door, and they were on their way.

The ride to Andy's house was warm and cozy. Daisy's best feature was her heater; it kept the inside of the car comfortably toasty. The easy conversation they shared, so different from their disastrous

141

beginning, made Andy feel content and gave the fall night a rosy glow. Daisy didn't have bucket seats, so when Joe patted the seat next to him, Andy slid over to his side unquestioningly. He slipped his arm gently around her shoulder, and she leaned her head against him. It felt perfect to be right where she was.

Joe explained about his family and how he was the first of Kevin Duffy's children to go to college. They had been very proud of him when he'd received his scholarship to Bayshore University. He would be the first Dr. Duffy in the entire family. He told her again how much he wanted to be a doctor, a pediatrician; how much he loved medicine; and how much he loved kids.

As they rode down the dark streets, comfortable in the cozy car and each other's company, Joe seemed to want to tell her all about himself, his dreams, his fears, and his hopes.

Andy wanted nothing more than to lean against him contentedly and listen. He would be a wonderful doctor. She knew that now. And pediatrics was the perfect field for Joe. She still didn't think he'd be the same kind of children's doctor Daniel Stewart was. He would be every bit as good—just different. The words that John had said to her in jest leaped into her mind: she would love to be Joe Duffy's special nurse. She would love to be Joe Duffy's special . . . something.

The house on Fourteenth Street was dark; no light shone in any of the windows or on the porch when they pulled into the driveway. That was strange. Big Andy always waited up for her to get home from a date. And he always left the light on the front porch burning, as a kind of warning. It reminded her dates not to tarry too long at her door. Like every father, she guessed, he worried about his daughter until she was safely tucked into her own bed. Then it dawned on her. He wasn't worried about her because she was out with Joe. Big Andy liked Joe. He trusted him. He even knew Joe's family. Leaving the porch light off was his way of letting her know that he approved of Joe. Andy felt a rush of love for her father at that moment. He'd known, regardless of the words she'd said, that she approved of Joe, too. It had just taken her until tonight to find it out.

As Andy stood with Joe on the patio, she could have hugged her dad for his silent message, but what she really wanted—was to kiss Joe.

Taking her key from her pocket, she unlocked the front door quietly. "Would you like to come in for a while?"

"Uh-huh. But I won't. You have to work the early shift tomorrow, and I have a seminar bright and early at seven o'clock. But I want to. More than anything, I want to. Well . . . almost more than anything."

"Oh?" Her heart was doing acrobatics again.

"What I really want more than anything is this. . . ."

Andy felt herself lifted off the ground and into his arms. He held her pressed against his chest. She could feel the steady thundering of his heartbeat in tempo with her own. Slowly he lowered his head, and she closed her eyes. When his lips touched hers, everything else stopped. The world stood still for Andy. Behind her closed lids, the glow of a thousand starbursts, brighter than a million porch lights left burning, lit up her heart.

Joe took his lips from hers and the lights dimmed, but they didn't go out. Even after she opened her eyes, the shimmering stars remained.

"Good night, Andy." Joe's voice was a husky whisper.

"Good night, Joe. And thank—"

He silenced her words with a feather-light brush of his lips against hers. "Thank *you.*"

The starlight danced and flickered.

He pushed open the door, waited until she stepped into the house, and then pulled it closed behind her.

Andy automatically turned the locks and floated down the hallway to her bed.

A Good News Day

"I WAS BEGINNING to think that Professor Arnold would never stop talking and let us out of class. I don't know how he does it, but he never manages to run out of words—until five minutes after dismissal," complained Liz.

"Huh? I guess I didn't notice," answered Andy absentmindedly.

"So I noticed. Well, I'm all ears, child. Tell Lizzie all about it."

"About what?"

"About what you find so interesting that even devastatingly boring Professor Arnold can't hold your attention. You know what I want to hear—about your date with Joe Duffy. I was right about him, wasn't I? Doesn't Joe make a lot more sense for you than your silly crush on Dr. Dan?"

"Liz, for Pete's sake, I don't have a crush or anything else on Dr. Daniel Stewart."

"I'm glad to hear it. And now it's definitely true love between you and Joe. I knew it would be," Liz gloated.

"I don't know about love, but it's definitely true like," confided Andy. "I really do like him. He's fun and he's nice."

"So tell me what you two did after you left Jackee and Monica in Westwood. Where'd he take you?"

"Boy, news sure travels fast around here. You've already had the full report from the Margarita Street contingent. He took me to an old Irish pub in West L.A. It's called Duff's.''

"Is that Duff's as in Duffy?" Liz grinned, as if she'd suddenly guessed Andy's most intimate secret.

"Yes. As in Duffy, Sherlock Jones. Joe's family owns the pub and restaurant."

"Well, that's serious stuff, you know. A guy doesn't take just anybody home to meet his mother, not to mention his entire family— unless, of course, he means business."

"Come on, Liz. It was just one date. How serious is that? What kind of business does one date mean?"

"Monkey business? Let me see your right hand," requested Liz. Without waiting, she grabbed Andy's hand and turned it palm up, then back, inspecting it carefully before letting go.

"What in heaven's name are you looking for?" asked Andy.

"The place where Joe rubbed off all that skin holding hands with you in the movie. I wanted to see if it had regenerated itself yet," teased Liz. "Thought I might do a paper on it: 'Secondhand Research into Friction Burns from the Fire of Love.' ''

Andy slipped her hands behind her back. "All right, that's enough of that. Joe didn't rub off any of my skin. He was just holding hands a little, that's all. Jackee has two big eyes and too big an imagination," insisted Andy with a scowl.

"You're right. And I'll bet he didn't even kiss you one time. Did he? Never mind; you don't have to answer that. I can read the answer on your beautiful red face."

"I am not red. Absolutely nothing happened between Joe and me to make me blush."

"Then all of that vivid color must be due to old Arnold's stimulating lecture."

Andy glared at her friend, hoping she looked as exasperated as she felt. Couldn't she have any secrets? Her friends must be running an N.I.T. underground; information about her was distributed so fast!

"Honest, you didn't miss anything important," said Liz as they skirted the parking lot. "We were just discussing the vital, life-

145

changing ramifications of bypass heart surgery on the aged. You remember learning something about them, don't you?''

"Of course, I remember. Quit clowning, Liz."

"And do you remember Arnold's theories on the stats for a positive full-life recovery in patients over sixty?''

"Sure I do. Everyone over the age of sixty who has bypass heart surgery has the optimum possibilities of . . . um. . . .'' Andy reluctantly admitted to herself that she really hadn't been paying as much attention to the professor's lecture as she should have.

"Of living happily ever after? Right? Forget it, girl. I'm afraid love's given you fuzzy, nonfunctioning gray matter today.''

Andy knew there was no use wasting her breath trying to convince Liz of anything Liz didn't want to be convinced of. And she wasn't so sure her friend was that far off. It had been handsome twenty-one-years-young Joe Duffy, not some unknown sixty-year-old heart patient, occupying her thoughts during Professor Arnold's class.

The emergency entrance to the hospital seemed to loom up out of nowhere. Andy had been so engrossed in her discussion with Liz that she hadn't noticed the time passing, as they crossed the expansive university campus.

"Your stop first. 'Bye, Liz," said Andy.

"*Ciao*. Try to remember, will you? All Joe and no work makes a grim Grymes," called Liz. With a quick wave she disappeared into Emergency.

Andy smiled to herself. Was Liz right about Joe? Did he mean business? She went through the main entrance of the hospital, crossed the lobby, and stepped into the elevator without feeling her feet touch the ground. At the third floor, she drifted through the open elevator doors and floated down the hall like a weightless astronaut. Joe Duffy, Joe Duffy, Joe Duffy, said the squish, squish, squish of her rubber-soled shoes as they glided across the highly polished tile.

She was well beyond the door to Dr. Dan's office before she even noticed she'd passed it. This was the first time that she could remember passing his door without thinking of him. She brushed away that brief thought. There was no room in her head or her heart for any man—except Joe.

146

"Andréa? Andréa, would you mind coming into my office for a moment?"

The sound of Dr. Dan's voice, so soon after the realization that she could forget all about him, was startling. But she had to admit that he did have a way of saying her name that pleased her.

"Of course. Coming right now, Doctor."

He held his office door open for her, and she stepped in past him. There were two people sitting in front of Dr. Dan's desk with their backs to Andy. One she recognized as Dr. Fricker. The other, a woman, had her head down. When Andy entered, the woman turned to look at her. She was wearing the trim navy blue and crisp white-collared uniform of a policewoman.

"Miss Whitman." She acknowledged Andy in a serious-sounding voice.

"Hello." Andy looked from Dr. Dan to Dr. Fricker questioningly. Why was she here? What would a policewoman want from her?

"Please sit down, Andrea," said Dr. Fricker, pointing to the seat he'd just vacated.

"I'm fine, Doctor. I can stand, really," mumbled Andy. She felt confused.

The kindly doctor nodded and sat down again.

"Andréa," Dr. Dan's voice was somber, "although I'm sure that you'd rather not speak about it, I want you to tell Officer Rae everything that Heather said to you before her tonsillectomy."

"Please, Dr. Dan, I don't want to—to remember that day," stammered Andy.

"We understand how you feel, dear," Dr. Fricker comforted. "But Officer Rae has to know. You can tell her what Heather won't. It will help the authorities make the right decision."

What decision? wondered Andy. Wouldn't telling what had happened cause Heather more pain?

"I—I can't, sir." What about Heather's rights?

"Andréa, please. Sit in my chair. I'd never ask this of you if it weren't gravely important."

Andy lowered herself into Dr. Dan's high-backed chair. She felt

147

small and insignificant sitting there behind his huge oak desk. She looked from one doctor to the other. Both smiled back at her, but their faces contained stern expressions and sad eyes.

"Miss Whitman? Andrea?"

Andy looked at Officer Rae.

"Andrea, you will have to tell me," the officer said. "Before we can help Heather, we have to have a full report."

"Don't be afraid. We're all concerned about Heather." Dr. Dan's voice was reassuring.

"Our report requires only that you state the events as they happened. We can't include any opinion in our report to the courts," said the officer. "Start from the first day Heather was admitted and continue right up to today. Tell us what Heather said to you. Include any changes in her condition and when they happened, any unusual occurences during her hospitalization. That kind of thing, but only observed facts. No supposition."

"What's going to happen to Heather?"

"The courts will make that decision when they know all the facts in the case. Heather may be put in a foster home for a while, and her mother will receive help. Different cases are handled in different ways," said Officer Rae. "In every case, the child is the most important consideration."

Andy thought back. Heather seemed petrified of her mother. Love and hate; there was such a thin line between them. Hesitantly she related her experiences with the little girl who was under her care.

"Are you sure Heather will be all right? What will happen to Mrs. Berk?" asked Andy when she had finished.

Dr. Dan and Dr. Fricker explained life crisis counseling and the family services program that Bayshore's Crisis Center provided. They'd helped many parents learn to cope with the frustrating circumstances that often led to child abuse. And they'd accompanied many a child down the path of recovery from the trauma of abuse.

"Thank you, Miss Whitman," said Officer Rae. "We'll have to put this report in writing. For the time being you can go. I'll be getting back to you."

Andy left the room and closed the door noiselessly behind her.

She was glad it was over. She suddenly felt very good again; Heather was going to be all right.

That feeling lasted two minutes. She looked at her watch. She'd forgotten to check in, and the figure who was steamrolling her way down the corridor was Simon LeGrymes. No matter how legitimate a reason she had for being late, Andy knew it was going to fall on deaf supervisor ears. Mrs. Grymes had a way of making her feel very guilty, even when there was nothing to feel guilty about. Andy didn't know how Mrs. Grymes did it, but she did. She braced herself for the attack.

"There you are, Andrea."

"Yes, ma'am. I know I'm a little late checking in, but I really couldn't help it. I was in Dr. Dan's office. He called me in to talk to a policewoman. Dr. Fricker was—"

"I understand, Andrea. Please don't worry about it. There weren't any emergencies that the other nurses couldn't handle. And I thoroughly enjoyed filling in for you at story time."

"You did?" Mrs. Grymes had actually read stories to the kids? For her? Andy felt light-headed.

"Is everything okay? In Dr. Stewart's office, I mean?"

"Oh, yes. Fine now, Mrs. Grymes," Andy murmured, unsure of what to make of *this* Mrs. Grymes. Surely this wasn't the same supervisor she'd had the day before. This was a "Twilight Zone" trick someone was playing on her. They'd substituted this friendly, smiling platinum blonde clone for the real Mrs. Grymes. Well, I won't be the one, Andy decided quickly, to give away the perpetrators of this fiendish plot. I intend to enjoy it.

"I know that what you've just gone through had to have been hard for you, Andrea."

Andy nodded and stared.

"And I think you just might be in the mood for some extra special good news. What do you think?"

Andy nodded again, speechless.

"The hospital board of directors," said Mrs. Grymes very slowly, "has unanimously voted"—she dragged it out—"to support you and your project for painting the children's rooms."

149

"They have? They said yes? We can do it?" Andy was ecstatic. She grabbed her supervisor and happily hugged her. Then, remembering who it was she hugged, she let go quickly and stepped back.

"Yes. And what's more, they've even awarded you a small budget to help you buy your supplies. Oh, there is one little thing. They did ask to see preliminary sketches of the planned paintings before you begin. In fact, I'm rather eager to see the sketches too. I want to get first choice of what I'm going to paint." Mrs. Grymes put her arms around Andy and squeezed her. "The children are going to love having a marina, Sea Cove Landing, the beach, and the birds inside their rooms." The supervisor barreled away leaving Andy standing in the middle of the hall, elated and open-mouthed.

Project Paint-It

FIRST RING: LEAP out of the bathtub and grab a towel. *Second ring:* wrap the towel sarong-style and start to run. *Third ring:* leave wet footprints across the powder blue bedroom carpeting and grab the phone—quick.

"You sound out of breath. Were you running? I didn't call at a bad time, did I?" asked Joe. His anxiously awaited voice raised goose bumps all over Andy's damp body.

"Oh, no. I wasn't doing anything important." There was no way she'd admit that from the moment she'd opened her eyes that morning she'd been hoping he'd call. And there was no way she'd admit that she'd jumped out of a warm bath just in case it was him on the phone. "I guess you got the note I left in the lab for you yesterday, before I went off duty," she said.

"You bet I did—the minute I walked in to work. You caused a quite a stir down there, you know. Everyone's been asking me who the great-looking doll was, looking for me."

"And did you tell them?"

"I did. I told them you were my girl, and it was strictly hands off. Pretty smart of me to get rid of the competition, wasn't it?"

"Absolutely ingenious," Andy agreed, glowing with pleasure.

"That was a very intriguing note you left me: 'If you believe that miracles can happen—call me. Love, Andy.' I not only believe; I didn't even wait for my break to call. I'm using the out-phone at the pediatric nurses' station. There's no one here now, but if I get caught—augh!''

"You must like miracles, because if Mrs. Grymes catches you using the nurses' phone, you'll need a miracle to save you."

"Oh, it's not the miracles I care about. I was intrigued by the 'Love, Andy' part. But you can tell me about the miracle anyway. But better make it fast!''

"They gave me permission to paint the kids' rooms. The hospital board said they thought it was a good idea. They even gave me a small—a very, very small—budget to get supplies. I won't be able to buy much, but—''

"That's fantastic, honey. But I knew they'd say yes. You've volunteered to do all the hard parts yourself. How could they lose?''

"But that's not all. There's even more. Mrs. Grymes said she wanted to see the sketches of what I was planning on painting so she could choose the subject she wanted to paint.''

"Now, that's a miracle,'' laughed Joe. His laughter sent tiny electrical charges to Andy's Joe-sensitive nerve endings.

"See? I told you.'' She joined him, laughing.

"Can you handle one more miracle?'' asked Joe.

"Try me. I'm ready for anything,'' insisted Andy.

"Remember when you first mentioned your painting project to me? And I told you about my uncle's paint store in Culver City?''

Andy held her breath. She was afraid to hope. "Uh-huh.''

"Well, I told him about your project, and I think I have some news that will brighten the hearts of your budget committee.''

"You're talking to the whole committee now, so brighten away.''

"My Uncle Sean happens to be the sole proprietor of Duffy's Isle O' Paints. And that happens to be the newest, biggest, fanciest paint store in Culver City's newest, biggest, fanciest shopping mall. He would like to do something to help the kids and their pretty N.I.T., if you'd let him.''

"Oh, Joe! That's so wonderful. You're so wonderful. Joe?''

"What's the matter? Aren't I wonderful anymore?'' Joe asked.

152

He sounded disappointed that her enthusiasm had come to such an abrupt end.

"You know you are. But how does your Uncle Sean know that the kids have a pretty N.I.T.?"

"Because he trusts the judgment of his darlin' nephew Joe. And because that description was confirmed by eight other Duffys. And because I'm one of his favorite nephews. . . ."

"How many favorite nephews does your uncle have?"

"Eighteen."

"How many nephews does he have all together?"

"Eighteen."

"I thought as much. Joe Duffy, you're so full of blarney, I can hardly believe it," teased Andy.

"One of the finer traits I've inherited, being a Duffy. When we have kids, they'll have the talent too."

Andy's heart skipped a beat. For the tiniest moment she let herself think about being Joe's wife and about their kids. But she quickly dismissed the thought. He was probably joking with her again. Someday she would pay Joe back for always teasing her so. "What about your uncle's paint store?" she said, reminding him.

"Right. Uncle Sean always says he has plenty of old stock he'd like to donate to a worthy cause. Anything else we need—you need, that is—he'll give to us at cost."

"Really? Joe, that's so—"

"Can't talk any longer. Grymes is on the horizon. I'm off work at two this afternoon. Can you go with me to Uncle Sean's?"

"Absolutely," Andy answered quickly.

"Pick you up at two-thirty. . . . Mrs. Gadjuwonsky? You must have the wrong floor, ma'am. No one in pediatrics by that name." The phone went dead in Andy's hand.

Two-thirty! Only four more hours to get ready. What should I wear? What would be perfect for a fancy paint store?

Duffy's Isle O' Paints was located in one of those sprawling outdoor shopping centers that Southern California was so famous for.

Any one of the lovely redwood stores would have made a fantastic house to live in on a bluff in Santa Monica or at Malibu Beach.

Joe held Andy's hand as he led the way down one of the terra cotta paths, through a garden in the center court, and then across the small wooden bridge that spanned the mall's miniature river.

"You were right about your uncle's paint store. I've never seen one this beautiful. This whole center is so lovely, I wouldn't mind living here," said Andy, making a little pirouette so she could see everything.

"No one but Uncle Sean would want to live in there. It always smells like fresh paint."

It was a typical fall day in California—not too cold and not too warm; a light-sweater day. Tourists came to the West Coast for its warm summers or its mild winters, but the locals knew that autumn was the best and tried to keep it a secret from everyone else. Uncle Sean knew the secret; the paint store doors were opened wide to let in the lovely autumn day.

Joe scanned the store for his uncle and shook his head. "I don't see Uncle Sean anywhere," he reported.

"Your uncle must do a wonderful business. There are so many busy salesmen. Maybe your uncle just decided to take the day off," suggested Andy.

"No, he didn't go home. Uncle Sean wouldn't miss meeting you for the world. Not after what I told him about you."

"What terrible things did you say, Joe Duffy?" She gave him her fiercest scowl.

"The worst. But after the glowing report he got from Mom and Pop, he didn't believe a thing I said." Joe slipped an arm around her waist and squeezed her.

"Could we just look around before your uncle gets here?" Before he could answer, she grabbed his hand and began pulling him down the closest aisle.

"Here. Stick this on," Andy said gleefully. She plopped a white cotton painter's cap on Joe, with the cardboard visor in the back. She put one on, too. "They'll make us look much more professional."

"Professional? I feel like a dodo," griped Joe, playfully tipping his cap.

"Exactly. Like professional dodos. What else?" teased Andy.

"On you it looks kind of cute," he teased back, making a face.

"Oh, look at all those lovely brushes and cans of paint and these racks of gorgeous color chips," said Andy, overjoyed.

"And these lovely drop clothes. And these exciting, furry rollers. And did you see this stunning can of paint thinner? It's all too marvelous. It really is," Joe gently teased her enthusiasm.

"Joe Duffy, you're terrible," Andy sputtered. Her excitement wasn't dampened in the least. "I even love these wallpaper samples. Everything here is beautiful. I want one of each."

"May I help you?" asked the man in the green jacket who mysteriously appeared beside them.

Andy jumped. Where had he come from? she wondered.

"No, thank you," began Joe. "We're just. . . . Oh, Uncle Sean!"

Andy knew immediately that he was Uncle Sean. The redheaded man was definitely kith and kin to Kevin Duffy, but like Joe and John, he had all the height that Kevin Duffy didn't. As Joe put it, all the Duffy men were either giants or leprechauns. There was no in-between.

"Uncle Sean, I'd like you to meet Andrea Whitman, the nurse I told you about. You can call her Andy, if you'd like."

"So, shall I? How does Andy suit you, darlin'?" he asked.

"I don't mind—at all. If you'd like to, Uncle Sean . . . I mean, Mr. Duffy," stammered Andy.

"Then we'll make a pact. You'll always be Andy to me. But I have to be Uncle Sean to you. Deal?"

"Deal . . . Uncle Sean." Suddenly Andy found herself swallowed up in an exuberant hug that included the smallest hint of an Irish jig. All the Duffys are wonderful, she decided.

Joe and his uncle talked briefly about the well-being of Joe's family and exchanged quips and jokes accompanied by friendly pats on the back.

"Come with me into the back, kids," Uncle Sean said.

She and Joe followed him through the doors that led to the crowded rear of the store. The front of the store had impressed Andy, but the back overwhelmed her. It was a beggar's paradise. There were rolls of things, piles of things, stacks of things, heaps, shelves, boxes, and barrels of marvelous things for her to pick through.

"Joe, anything in this area is yours for the taking. You and Andy take all the time you need. Pick out as much as you like. I'll be out front trying to keep the help honest, if you need me." He smiled warmly at them, then went back into the main part of his store.

"Uncle Sean's in love. Could you tell?" asked Joe.

"I would have thought that he was already married and had a dozen kids. He's such a sweet man and so much like your father."

"Oh, he is. He's been married to Aunt Eve for almost forty years. Uncle Sean's a father six times over, a grandad eleven times more. And it's only a matter of days, before he and Aunt Eve will be the great-grandparents of twins. My cousin Mary Florence's daughter Maya is due any minute."

"Then I don't believe a word of it. With a big, lovely family like that, your uncle would never fall in love with someone else. Joe Duffy, it's getting so I can't believe a word you say."

"Believe it or not, Uncle Sean has caught the same fatal lovesickness the rest of the Duffys have. Every one of them is in love with a certain Andy Whitman. She's a nurse-in-training at Bayshore Medical Center. Ever heard of her?"

"Never. Do you really mean *all* the Duffys, Joe?"

"Every single one," he whispered, leaning over to brush her soft cheek with his lips.

Joyful shivers raced through her body. "I'm awfully glad, Joe," she told him quickly, before her courage could escape. "I think I've fallen in love with *all* the Duffys too."

"Have you, Andy? Are you sure?" Without speaking he gathered her into his arms and pulled her willingly toward him.

Her legs turned to marshmallow, and she would have slipped to the floor, but his arms held her too tightly. Andy slipped her arms around Joe's neck, and she clung to him. Her heart felt as if it were touching his. She was drowning in new sensations, from his touch, his nearness. When at last his soft lips met hers, waves of delirious happiness broke over her, blotting out the rest of the world. For Andy there was only Joe, the gentle crush of his lips on hers, the awakening passions of first love.

"You have a smudge on your nose," Joe said breathlessly, as he slowly lifted his lips from hers.

"So do you," whispered Andy. She'd opened her eyes to find him staring at her with disturbing intensity.

"On the very tip. Here." He kissed the end of her nose for emphasis. "I love you, Andy Whitman."

"And I love you, Joe Duffy."

"More than all the other Duffys?"

"More than all the other Duffys."

"How's it going, you two? Did you find everything you wanted?" called Uncle Sean from the doorway.

Andy and Joe continued to stare into each other's eyes, each too filled with the wonder of love to look away. It was as if they shared the same thoughts. As if they'd found a special way to communicate silently through a magical force known only to lovers. In unspoken unison they nodded. They had found everything they wanted: they'd found each other. The cardboard visors on their forgotten painters' caps agreed, too. They bobbed up and down on the back of their heads.

Many Hands and a Few Surprises

TODAY WAS THE big day—Robbie's surprise day—painting day! Robbie and his new roommate, Jared Chadwick, were moved, beds and all, to another room on pedi-3. Heather had left a few days before for her new life in a temporary foster home.

Even though it was her day off and she could have slept in, Andy planned to reach the hospital a good hour before the regular routine in pediatrics would begin. She was too excited to sit at home waiting for the clock to tell her it was time to leave for the eight o'clock bus. Her eyes had sprung open at four o'clock, and they'd insisted on staying open.

Big Andy was working the dawn patrol as he called it, and she could hear him banging around in the other bathroom getting ready to leave. "Dad, could you drop me at the hospital on your way to work?" she called.

"Sure, honey," he answered. "Glad to have the company. You'll brighten up my morning."

Andy decided she was glad she couldn't sleep. She was eager to start her special project, but also happy to have a few, special unexpected minutes with her dad.

"What are you supposed to be?" he asked, as he entered the kitchen. "That can't be what this year's well-dressed nurse is wearing?" he teased.

She poured him a cup of tea and sat across from him at the kitchen table. "Dad, you know perfectly well that I'm wearing painter's whites, not nurse's whites. You're a big tease."

He chuckled. "Do you think you could use a big tease's helping hand today? I could come by after I get off duty."

"Dad, that would be terrific. We can use all the help we can get. Besides, I'd like to have my dad there."

Big Andy pushed back his chair and stood up. He leaned across the table and kissed his daughter on the forehead. "And he'd like to be there, Blossoms."

It had been a long time since he'd called her by the name he'd helped her pick out when she was six and in Indian Maidens. It was something special between them. She kissed him back.

"I'll grab some old painting clothes and meet you at the car." He put down his cup with a bang and took off for the bedroom.

While Andy rinsed the two mugs, she thought about her mom. She'd be happy if she knew how much Little Andy and Big Andy loved each other, but sad if she knew how much they both missed her. She dried the cups and her hands, picked up her painter's cap from the entryway table, then went out to wait for Big Andy.

Word of her painting project had spread to every floor of the hospital. Volunteers popped up everywhere. Those who couldn't help immediately, because they were on duty or had a class, promised to come back as soon as they could. There was no distinction made between doctors, nurses, technicians, N.I.T.s, or supervisors. Any and all offers were gratefully accepted.

At eight-thirty, the time they'd agreed to meet, Joe bounded into the nurses' lounge exuding enough enthusiasm and energy to paint the Bayshore Medical Center complex—all by himself. He hurtled, more than walked, over to Andy, who was trying to sort the ton of painting supplies into some semblance of order. Either he didn't notice Jackee kneeling in the middle of a pile of old drop cloths, or he just didn't care if she saw him or not; but he lifted Andy off her feet, swung her around in the air, and kissed her long and loud before putting her down.

"Ah love. Ain't it grand," Jackee mooned, sounding wistful.

"You are so right, Jack, my girl," said Joe, fairly crowing with happiness. He bent down and gave her a noisy peck on the cheek. "That'll have to hold you until you find a fella of your own."

"Stop flirting with my friend. Soon to be my ex-friend—if she doesn't stop flirting with my guy," teased Andy. "Did you come here to work, Joe? Or to break up friendships?"

"To work, you slave driver," he retorted.

"I don't want to hear another word about slaves," Liz announced, swinging through the lounge door. "My people don't take kindly to it." Her stern look was immediately replaced by a carefree smile, as she greeted her friends.

"Whatever we do, we don't want to antagonize Liz," Andy whispered too loudly. "She's promised to sketch the master plan for—"

"What plan did you say?" asked Liz with a giggle.

"The overall *major* plan for the picture we're going to paint. Better?" asked Andy, smiling at Liz.

Liz threw her arms around Andy and hugged her tightly. "You've got class, girl." She gathered up the mass of preliminary sketches she'd helped Andy draw.

"You know what you've got?" asked Jackee, holding up one of the many sheets of drawing paper. "You've got real artistic ability, Liz." Jackee and Liz joined hands and did a few quick dance steps across the room. "But no rhythm!" They collapsed against each other in a fit of giggles.

"You two get serious. We've got a lot to do today," warned Andy.

"Better listen up, ladies. Andrea Whitman is a bear of a boss," joked Joe.

Andy added emphasis to his words with a loud growl.

"We're going. We're going," Liz and Jackee shouted at the same time. Filling their arms with supplies, they danced from the lounge, laughing hysterically and saying something that sounded like, "Please don't eat us, Bossy Bear. Please don't eat us."

"I like your friends more every day," said Joe.

"So do I," agreed Andy. She filled her arms with drop cloths, paint rollers, mixing paddles, and brushes. "Well?" she asked Joe, pointedly.

"Well? You seem to be doing fine all by yourself, my little Handy Andy." He reached over and tickled her playfully.

"You stop messing around; you're going to make me drop all these things. Instead of making trouble, Joe Duffy, make yourself useful."

He leaned over and kissed her on the tip of her nose. "No smudge today," he noted, then picked up a ladder and followed her to room four.

Several more volunteers arrived as they were dumping the first load of supplies and starting to go back for the second. Andy decided to remain in room four and let Joe supervise the transfer of the painting materials from the lounge to the painting site.

"That's everything, Andy, except for the long board from the university's theater arts department. We need it for a catwalk," said Joe.

"What's a catwalk?" Monica asked seriously. She was on her break and had stopped in to check on the painters' progress. She was on morning duty and couldn't join the painting party until three.

"This is a catwalk." With a paint paddle in each hand, Jackee pranced across the room, swishing her make-believe, feline tail behind her. She circled the drop cloth, meowing with every step. "You, roomie dear, of all people—the world's biggest lover of four-legged, furry felines—you should know how a cat walks."

Monica took one of the paint paddles and gave her roommate a gentle swat. "Come on. I really want to know."

"It's a board you put between two ladders—from one top step to the other—and then you can walk back and forth and paint anything that's too high to reach from the floor. House painters use them all the time," Joe explained.

"So do artistic cats," teased Jackee.

161

"They call it a catwalk because you have to walk with the light step and surefooted grace of a cat," added Andy, giving Jackee a "now that's enough" look.

"Not to mention the importance of landing on your feet, like a cat, if you fall off," said Liz, balancing on an imaginary tightrope and swaying dangerously.

"Or praying you still have eight lives to go—if you you land on your head?" asked Monica, joining in on their silly jokes.

"Now you've got it." Joe laughed and shook Monica's hand with the Kevin Duffy arm-pumper-special that Andy remembered so well.

"Thanks, everyone, for the fascinating introduction to the fine art of house painting. I'd better get back; my babies need me. I'll see you at three," Monica called. She had to step around Mrs. Grymes to get out of the room.

"I still don't know what to do about the catwalk. It won't fit in the elevator. There's no way to get the thing up to the third floor," complained Joe, scratching his head thoughtfully.

"Think again, Mr. Duffy. You're a big, strong young man. Haven't you ever heard of using the stairs?" asked Mrs. Grymes.

Joe groaned.

The male nurse from OR, who'd been helping Joe carry in the heavier things, didn't say a word. He was too busy trying to slip out the door behind Mrs. Grymes.

"You, too, Mr. Casadio." The supervisor stopped him in his tracks. "It won't hurt you to lend Duffy a hand."

"That's just where I was headed, Mrs. Grymes." Paulo Casadio took off on the run.

Mrs. Grymes looked at Joe.

"Me, too, ma'am," he mumbled. Following Paulo's lead, he raced through the open door.

"How is everything coming along, Andrea?" asked the supervisor.

"We should be ready to begin painting soon. We've got all the equipment moved in, and Joe's getting the catwalk. By lunch, we'll be ready to begin the actual painting. Don't you think so, Liz?"

162

Andy turned to survey the section of wall where Liz was sketching her sailboats in broad, sure strokes.

Liz nodded. She couldn't answer Andy with words; her mouth was filled with artist's pencils.

"I look forward to doing my bit," Mrs. Grymes said jauntily. "Painting is my second love. Of course, nursing is first."

"Yes, Mrs. Grymes," chorused Andy, Jackee, Liz, Susie from maternity, and Dina Johnson. There was a silence as they looked at each other and barely contained their smiles. Laugh at Mrs. Grymes? Not even Dina dared do that.

"Around lunch time, then," promised the supervisor before bustling out the door.

For a moment the room was so still that Mrs. Grymes's sensible shoes, moving off down the hall, made the only sound the girls heard. Then a small giggle crept out between Dina's lips. Soon all five nurses were crying tears of laughter.

"Right, left, hup, hup. What's the matter with you, Joe? Can't you keep up?" called Paulo, carrying the front end of the catwalk into the room.

"You can't talk to me like that. I just happen to be the managing director in charge of supply deployment. I decide when we step with the right foot and when we step with the left. And I think my hup broke on the second-floor landing." Joe followed Paulo into the room, the back end of the long board resting on one broad shoulder. "You tell him, Andy. I'm a boss. I have a title. Some people ain't got no respect."

"That's not fair, Andy. If Joe has a title, I get one too," moaned Paulo.

"Seems only right, doesn't it?" added Liz, standing back to view her sketches.

"To me, too," agreed Dina.

Susie and Jackee nodded.

"What would you like to be in charge of, Paulo?" asked Andy.

"I'd like to be the managing director in charge of direction—the left-right-hup guy."

"You've got it," announced Andy. "In fact, while I run down to the lounge to get us some coffee, I think it would be a wonderful idea if you all gave yourselves titles. Jackee, you already know mine.''

"I do?'' Jackee looked up from mixing paint.

"Bet you do—double or nothing? Shall I hum a few bars?''

Jackee laughed.

Joe frowned quizzically.

The others looked at each other with confused expressions.

Then, humming "All or Nothing at All,'' Andy went for the coffee.

In the lounge she filled the oversized thermos that Mrs. Grymes had brought in for the painting crew to use. Then, balancing the stacked Styrofoam cups, the sugar, the powdered cream, a dozen spoons, and twice that many napkins, she pushed open the lounge door with her shoulder, eased into the hallway, and walked into Dr. Dan.

"Whoa there,'' he said, grabbing her just before she fell at his feet—again. "Here, let me help you with that.'' He took the cups from her and placed them on top of a big, gray box he was carrying. "Now, all those sugar packets.''

Andy put the packets on the lid of the box; the rest was easy to manage.

"I'm sorry about bumping into you, Dr. Dan. I seem to do that a lot, don't I?''

"You aren't the only N.I.T. who seems to cross my path when I'm in it, Andréa, though I don't encounter you quite as often as I used to. I imagine that's because you're rarely alone anymore.''

She looked at him questioningly.

"More often than not, I see that nice young phlebotomist, Joe Duffy, holding you up.'' The doctor chuckled at his own joke.

Andy blushed.

"I was on my way to view the progress you're making with our mural. Oh, yes, and to bring you this small treat from my wife. Evie says she's sorry if she's sugar-poisoning all of you, but she wanted to do something to help. And I'm positive you're all working hard enough to burn them off, right?''

"Them?''

"The doughnuts. In the box."

"Doughnuts! Wonderful! Just what we needed. Tell Mrs. Stewart thank you." Andy stepped into room four, expecting to see her busy-bee painting crew burning up all that energy that Mrs. Stewart's doughnuts were supposed to replace. The room was empty. "I don't understand," she said, looking back at Dr. Dan. "I've been gone only a couple minutes. They were all here when I left."

From behind her in the hall, Andy heard the faint chant of "Right, left, right, left, hup, hup." It seemed to be getting louder. She peeked into the hall and laughed as a parade of painters pushed into the room past her.

"Where did you go?" Andy noted that there were more painters now than there had been before she went for the coffee.

"Recruiting," announced Mrs. Grymes, who arrived at the end of the line. "No one wanted to start painting until you returned. And when I stopped in and saw them all sitting around on their glutei maximi, I suggested they see who else was available to pitch in now or sign on for later."

"Most efficient of you, Mrs. Grymes," commented the doctor. He winked at Andy, then handed the doughnut box to Joe. Then he took the N.I.T. supervisor by the arm and led her out of the room.

"We even made pit stops," bragged Jackee. "See what good little helpers you have? What's in the box?"

"Doughnuts," said Andy. That was all she got out of her mouth before the roomful of starving artists attacked the box in Joe's hands.

When all the sweet, delicious crumbs had disappeared and all the cavernous appetites had been satiated, the actual painting got under way in earnest. When they wanted to, Andy's motley crew could function deftly as well as creatively.

There was a steady stream of visitors who took the time to drop in and offer approval, creative comment, and constructive advice. One nurse, who'd heard from Paulo what a great job they were doing, hurried down to view the project still dressed in her operating greens—cap, mask, gown, and all. She pulled a handful of swabs from a pocket under her gown and mopped the sweaty brows of the appreciative painters.

Sandwiches of all kinds, fruit, and other snacks were brought at steady intervals by all the hospital staff. Those who couldn't paint did their share in other ways. Nothing was turned down, and no one was turned away. There were times when room four was so filled with helpful, eager volunteers that it was really too crowded to paint. That didn't happen too often, though, and when it did, Andy seemed to work it out without insulting any of the budding artists.

Promptly at three o'clock Monica showed up with Gabby and her brother, Tonio. The painters were down to Andy, Joe, and Liz before their arrival. Andy wasted no time in putting the replacements to work.

The general opinion held by the three resident painters was optimistic. They all agreed that there was a good chance their mural masterpiece was actually ahead of schedule, but they weren't taking any chances. They continued working at a fast and steady pace.

"Now what?" asked Joe. "I've run out of sky to paint."

"Try a sailboat or a cloud," Liz suggested.

"I do my best work with a roller, Liz. If you value your sketches, I'd better stick to big, wide, one-color surfaces."

"I never let things being one color stop me, and neither should you. I'm about to give you a much-needed lesson in cooperation. Here!" Liz shoved a wide brush covered with white paint into Joe's hand. "See that cloud? Paint."

"But Liz."

"But nothing. Paint!"

Joe painted. He carefully stayed inside the lines. He worked a little bit slower on clouds than he did on sky, but he filled in each one neatly. He looked at Liz and beamed.

"You're not done yet so save that charming, boyish grin." Liz took the first brush and replaced it with a thin one and a can of gray paint. Joe held the smaller brush in his hand, and she held Joe's hand in hers. With expressive and sweeping motions, she guided his path around the curves of one cloud. The still wet white paint blended with the gray. A soft little cloud came alive under Joe's touch. For his next artistic effort, Liz decided he was ready to go it alone. Soon Joe was dipping and swirling with ease. He created all the delicate shadows exactly as Liz had shown him. He became deeply involved in his clouds.

"Andy, come see my masterpiece," he called out excitedly.

Andy honestly had to admire Joe's work. Liz was as good a teacher as she was an artist. Andy gave Joe a big kiss on the cheek. In no time he would be ready for a much more difficult assignment, she told him. She vetoed his suggestion to add bikini-clad sunbathers.

"How about eyes on the clams?" asked Tonio. "I think—"

Suddenly the large window on the opposite wall began to vibrate. The rattling became dangerously louder.

"Earthquake!"

No one could remember who had shouted the first warning, but that didn't matter. In a hospital, the staff undergoes many different safety drills to prepare them for every type of emergency. In a California hospital, earthquake drills are routine.

But flying paint is not routine. Joe lunged for the catwalk, rescuing his gray paint with only inches to spare. It took barely a moment to survey the other painting supplies and see that there was no danger of any paint cans getting spilled in the event of an aftershock. Then, as quickly as possible, everyone ran into the corridor to offer their help.

"Just comfort the kids," called Mrs. Grymes. "So far, there's been no report of any serious damage." She disappeared into one of the wards.

The N.I.T.s, Joe, and Tonio separated. Each headed for a different room. No one at Bayshore needed to be told what to do.

Much to the credit of the entire pediatric staff, it took less than thirty minutes to restore calm to the floor. They'd hardly left before the painters were back at work.

"What is this supposed to be?" Andy pointed and demanded indignantly. "Since when does a rainbow have a big glob of gray in it?"

"Since Joe took up painting," teased Gabby.

"Since an earthquake decided to give me a hand painting the

clouds," answered Joe. "Get back to work on that octopus, Gabby."

Gabby made a face at him and turned back to her painting.

"Can we fix the rainbow, Liz, so no one will know what a lousy painter Joe really is?" Andy teased.

"Why, you little—" He made a quick grab for her.

She ducked under his arm to escape his second try, almost knocking Mrs. Grymes into the cerulean paint can. "Excuse me. I didn't see you, Mrs. Grymes," offered Andy, trying her best to apologize.

"Everyone seems to have handled our little disturbance quite nicely. The nursing staff has things running as smoothly as always. The children are, shall I say, unmoved and unworried by our tremor. But then, this *is* California."

The painters looked at one another and exchanged tentative smiles.

"It would appear that the only real excitement in pediatrics is in this room." Mrs. Grymes eyed Andy and Joe sternly. "I'm off duty in forty minutes. I'll change my clothes and return promptly. Perhaps a more mature attitude is required, if the painting is ever to get finished." Mrs. Grymes left in a flurry of rustling white.

"I think I need a break," said Joe. "Do I hear any takers for a quick bite in the cafeteria?"

"I could use a few minutes off my feet," agreed Monica.

"Me, too," said Gabby. "Come on, Tonio."

"And I could use a few minutes off my gluteus you-know-whateus. It's getting cramped from painting all those tiny shells at the bottom of the sea," Liz added.

"All I want to do is gear myself up for Monsoon Grymes, so when she hits our little painters' colony, a few of us survive the storm," laughed Andy, trooping out the door, too.

The sight that greeted Andy when she returned to her painting caused her mouth to gape and her head to spin. It wasn't possible, she thought.

Mrs. Grymes sat cross-legged in front of the mural, several paintbrushes in each hand and several more protruding from her mouth.

As she carefully—and with no small amount of expertise—applied the paint, her head nodded or shook depending on what her answer was to Big Andy's question. Beside her, shoulders nearly touching, sat Andy's dad dressed in his old gardening dungarees. He was meticulously dabbing paint where Mrs. Grymes pointed.

"Dad! You did come," cried Andy, happily.

"I told you I would. So, here I am." He and Mrs. Grymes stood up.

"You know everyone, don't you, Dad?" She eyed her supervisor suspiciously. "Lieutenant Andrew Whitman," introduced Andy.

"Not today, daughter. Today it's Lieutenant Andrew van Gogh."

Mrs. Grymes had removed the paintbrushes from between her teeth, and she laughed uproariously at Big Andy's joke.

"Big Andy Whitman, pride of the Venice Precinct, called Lieutenant Andrew van Gogh? Never!" Mrs. Grymes leaned against Andy's dad as if they were old friends. He put an arm around her shoulders, and they laughed together easily.

How could this delightful, giggling lady be the infamous Mrs. Grymes? But Andy heard it with her own two ears: Mrs. Grymes *giggled!* It's as if I'm seeing my supervisor for the very first time, she thought. She's never looked like this to me before. Andy tried to remember if she'd ever noticed that Mrs. Grymes had a very attractive figure. In that paint-spotted, tight-fitting jumpsuit, she did. And its soft pink went well with her fluffed platinum ringlets. Had her hair always been curled? wondered Andy. She hadn't noticed that, either. Or her light green eyes. Or her very tiny feet, now that she had exchanged her sensible nurses' shoes for some very unsensible sandals. There were so many things she hadn't noticed about her supervisor. Were they always there? Funny, Big Andy seemed to notice it all the first time he looked.

"Back to work, everyone," shouted Andy. She tried to sound as if she was in control and used her best benevolent-boss voice.

Before settling back down on the floor with her dad, Mrs. Grymes gave Andy a nod of approval and a broad smile. Andy wondered if it was her tone of voice she approved of, her in-control, I'm-the-boss voice. Or was it Big Andy?

* * *

At two minutes to midnight the last of the painting equipment had been cleared away, cleaned up, and stored for the next room the painters would embellish. A tired and satisfied group of people stood in room four to admire their art work. There were eleven people left at clean-up time, eleven yawning people.

"Andy, would you mind letting Joe drive you home?" asked Big Andy.

She was delighted, but it didn't make sense. She and Big Andy were going to the same house . . . or were they?

"I've offered to drive Esther home." Her father smiled at Mrs. Grymes, and she returned his warm expression, putting her hand on his arm.

"Thank you, Lieutenant Whitman, sir," said Joe, bowing to Big Andy and playing up his gratitude.

"Just don't keep her out on that cold front porch too long. And not too long on the warm couch, either. She has to work tomorrow," Big Andy reminded cheerfully.

Joe grabbed Andy's hand and quickly pulled her to the door. "You, too, sir. Mrs. Grymes needs her rest, too," he quipped, yanking Andy out of the room before Big Andy could retaliate.

"You coward," said Andy, tugging his ear gently.

"Oh, yeah?" He stepped into the water fountain alcove, dragging her after him. Instantly, his strong arms slid around her waist, holding her close. He lowered his head and their lips met in a fiery Fourth of July celebration.

"Kissing me doesn't take any courage, Joe Duffy."

"No, but waiting all day to do it does." He kissed her again.

170

18

Beyond Paradise

THE OCTOBER SUN was bright, but the breeze off the ocean had a crisp, wintery feeling, as it rustled the dried and fallen leaves. Joe held open Daisy's door and waited for Andy to climb in. They were going to Sea Cove Landing for a party on Liz's boat, the Chocolate Ship Cookie. And they were already late.

Sunday had arrived before Andy was prepared for it. The week of hospital work and classes, following room four's marathon mural painting, seemed to speed by. Her all-volunteer crew had done such a bang-up job, their talents were in demand not only by every child on pedi-3 but by every service that had a blank wall on every floor in the hospital. Liz was so busy sketching appropriate scenes for the long list of requested murals that she was toying with the idea of giving up her career in medicine to become a successful ar-tiste, as she pronounced it, full-time.

Every chance Andy had, she went into room four to admire the beautiful panorama she'd been so instrumental in having painted there. Even Robbie had been overwhelmed by the view they'd made for him.

"It's so bee-oo-tee-ful, Andy." Sitting on the edge of the bed that had belonged to Heather before she checked out, his chin resting on his hand, Robbie stared at the mural. "The picture is even better than the window. It's so bee-oo-tee-ful."

No matter how effusive the praises were, from the hospital staff or the many parents who were taken by their children to see the painting, Robbie's was the one word of praise Andy cherished the most.

Andy knew she hadn't painted Robbie's paradise alone, but it had been her idea, a creation of her mind and from her heart; she was satisfied.

"Hello, out there. Earth calling Andy. Earth to Andy," laughed Joe. "Are you going to waste all this wonderful sunshine on the one and only Sunday we'll have free together for a month, just standing on a curb and staring off into outer space?"

"Huh? No, I'm sorry. I was just thinking about the mural again. I'm so proud of it. I could look at it all day and not get tired of seeing it."

"It's a masterpiece, all right. But if you'd get into the car, we could make it to the real thing before it gets too dark to enjoy the sea, sun, and salty air. Hurry!"

Andy quickly climbed in, and Joe slammed the car door shut— twice, before it stayed shut.

The ride from Andy's house to Sea Cove Landing took less than twenty minutes; it was Andy's favorite drive. It took longer for them to pass the inspection at the Sea Cove guard gate than it did to get there. Even though the guard actually wrinkled his nose as he looked down it at Daisy, every "hmph" indicating that the Chevy didn't belong in such a classy neighborhood, Andy's and Joe's names were both on the visitor's list, and he had to let them pass.

Andy giggled at the man's disdain. "He probably can't afford a boat any more than we can. Just because he works at the Cove he's a snob."

"Liz should have warned me that they allow only expensive, classy automobiles through the gate," said Joe.

"I'm not ashamed of Daisy. She's a classic. And you've almost got her restored."

"I'm not ashamed of darlin' Daisy either; you know that. But I know where I could have borrowed a very sharp red Porsche. I hated to embarrass the guard." Joe winked at Andy.

She gave him a gentle poke in the ribs. It no longer mattered about

Collin. Mentioning him didn't embarrass Andy at all. If anything, she felt she should thank Collin Ellis; he'd brought them together. Collin had helped them fall in love.

"This is nice," admitted Andy a little reluctantly. She gazed out the window as Joe was parking the car. "Of course it's not as gorgeous as our mural—but nice." She watched the weekend sailors tack their boats back and forth across the wide channel as they zigzagged their way to open waters. The colorful spinnakers were beautiful, all bloated and billowing in the ocean breezes. To Andy they seemed like lovely rainbows skimming across blue glass. The snapping white mainsails and jibs of the smaller craft were like fleet-winged seabirds darting between the slower-moving, larger vessels. And the boats that Liz liked to refer to as "those smelly stinkpots," because they were power boats and not sailers like the Cookie, headed for the breakwater on arrow-straight courses at the channel's five-mile-per-hour speed limit, not dependent on the wind to propel them out to sea. Everywhere bright azure water sparkled and blinked to welcome Andy to Sea Cove Landing.

Joe's eyes shimmered with the same azure as he held the car door for Andy. She got out, and he took her hand. They walked together on the swaying dock toward the Chocolate Ship Cookie's slip. "Nice, huh? That's one of the reasons I love you so much—you're so humble. I love our mural too, honey. But this is a lot more than just 'nice.' This is real paradise."

"Uh-huh. Because I'm so humble—and what else?"

"What else, what?"

"What else do you love about me?"

"Your modesty?" he answered teasingly. They stopped short of their destination and leaned against the rail, gazing out at the gliding boats and the wheeling gulls. Joe sighed contentedly and held out his arms to her. Andy slid into them willingly.

We're the perfect couple, she thought. We fit together—perfectly. "You're a terrible tease, Joe Duffy. And that's one of the things I've learned to love about you." She looked up into his handsome face and knew her eyes were filled with her love for him.

"Oh, yeah? And what else?" he retorted with her own question.

173

"Oh, little things."

"Like what little things?"

"Like your hair." She ran her fingers slowly through his thick black curls. "I love your hair."

"Yours is softer. It shines as if it's spun with golden threads," he said.

"And your nose. It's so Grecian." Andy ran the tip of her finger down the bridge of his nose, ever so gently.

"Yours is pert and tiny as a bunny's, but twice as soft."

"And your lips. They're warm and gentle, and. . . ." Andy let her fingers trace a tingly path across his mouth.

He never got around to telling Andy why her lips were so much better than his own. With a soft moan he replaced her fingers with her lips. There was no need for him to say anything.

"Are you two coming aboard?" called Gabby from the gangplank of the Cookie. "Liz said to tell you that Sea Cove Landing's Official Committee for Public Decency frowns on that kind of behavior by unmarried people on their docks."

"We'd better stop," said Joe, continuing to deliver dozens of feather soft kisses all over Andy's mouth.

"Mmmm. We'll give the Landing a bad name," sighed Andy, snuggling closer into his arms.

"Then we'll just have to get married one of these days. So I can kiss you anytime and anyplace I want to," he whispered into her ear.

Andy trembled in Joe's arms. "Get married?" Her eyes glittered like rare emeralds when she finally dared to look up at him. Her heart throbbed happily, wildly, and madly out of control.

"I have a long way to go before I'm a doctor, Andy. I know we're going to have to wait. But it will happen. I love you so much. I want you forever and always. Will you wait with me, Andy? And will you marry me someday?" She'd never seen his face as serious as it was now. He gently brushed a stray curl from her forehead and kissed the spot where it had been.

"I love you, Joe. I can wait as long as it takes. I want you forever, too." The words were so easy to say and so easy to mean; they were said with her whole heart.

174

"I know this will qualify as more of Liz's unacceptable-in-public stuff. But if I don't kiss you again, this minute, I'll burst," Joe murmured.

Their lips met in a kiss that gave all the promises, expressed all the thoughts, and shared all the love that words never could.

Joe's kiss took Andy far beyond paradise.